A huge shadowy form...

Hap's eyes were sweeping the area. "Do you know what kind of cat kills a deer and buries it under grass and leaves? A mountain lion."

A surge of electrical currency crackled down my backbone. I shot a glance at Drover and noticed...gee, not much, just several dog hairs floating in the spot where he had been only seconds before. I mean, he had evaporated, poof, and was highballing it back to the machine shed.

My mouth had gone dry. "Wait a second. Are you saying..."

"We need to get out of here. Now."

"Hap, I'm giving the orders. On my mark, we will do an about-face and make an orderly..."

My words were obittilated...obiturated... phooey...my words were drowned by a SCREAM that made every hair on my back stand straight up, an unearthly scream full of horror and menace. Then...hang on...then a huge shadowy form crept toward us out of the trees...

The Case of the
Buried Deer

John R. Erickson

Illustrations by Gerald L. Holmes

Maverick Books, I

MAVERICK BOOKS, INC.

Published by Maverick Books, Inc.

P.O. Box 549, Perryton, TX 79070

Phone: 806.435.7611

www.hankthecowdog.com

First published in the United States of America by Maverick Books, Inc. 2019.

1 3 5 7 9 10 8 6 4 2

LIBRARY OF CONGRESS CONTROL NUMBER: 2019931124

978-1-59188-173-5 (paperback); 978-1-59188-273-2 (hardcover)

Hank the Cowdog® is a registered trademark of John R. Erickson.

Printed in the United States of America

To Keith and Nikki Earley.
God bless their home.

CONTENTS

Chapter One A Secret Mission For NASA **1**

Chapter Two Drover Robs a Train **9**

Chapter Three Bachelor Breakfast **17**

Chapter Four Bad News on the Radio **26**

Chapter Five Buzzards Arrive **36**

Chapter Six Food Freedom **47**

Chapter Seven A Gizzarly Problem **59**

Chapter Eight A Roadside Incident **67**

Chapter Nine Something Lurking
in the Machine Shed **77**

Chapter Ten You'll Never Guess What It Was **86**

Chapter Eleven Kitty Makes a Confession **95**

Chapter Twelve An Amazing Twist
in the Case, Wow! **105**

CHAPTER ONE

A Secret Mission For NASA

It's me again, Hank the Cowdog. Where should we start? Well, let's start at the beginning and see where that leads. I already know where it's going, but must be careful not to make scary statements about **CENSORED** or **CENSORED**.

See, I'm not allowed to mention the buried deer, not yet. We didn't find it until later, after I had almost been destroyed by something that was hiding in Slim's ice box, but I'm not allowed to talk about that one either. Classified.

For now, don't worry about it. There's no sense in watching the pot boil if you can't spill the milk.

The point is, the entire Security Division was covered up with work. Sleep? Forget it. Naps in

1

the afternoon? Ha. We're talking about double-shifts, no weekend passes, working days, nights, and holidays. We were being pushed to the limit.

It was late spring, as I recall, yes, the middle of May, and it had been a bad spring on my ranch. We had missed our early grass-growing rains and were in the second or third year of an awful drought.

Instead of getting April showers and May flowers, we'd gotten nonstop wind: hot wind, cold wind, north wind, south wind, west wind, wind from every direction except the one we wanted: east.

What's the big deal about an east wind? It brings moisture from somewhere, and it makes clouds that make rain. We weren't sure exactly how that process worked, but we knew one thing for certain: boy, we needed a rain!

In times of drought, our people get as cranky as badgers and can't talk about anything else. When they go to the feed store, they talk about bare pastures and dying trees. When they go to church, they complain about our dusty roads. When they go to a wedding, they say such things as, "Congratulations, and I hope it brings a rain."

The drought had put everybody in a bad mood, but there wasn't one thing we dogs could do about it. I mean, Drover and I had spent entire days barking at clouds, trying to shame them into forming up into decent thunderheads, but nothing had worked. We had tried every technique in the Cowdog Manual: Stern Barks, Coaxing Barks, Pleading Barks, and even Cloud-Rattling Barks. All our efforts amounted to zilch.

So it came as a huge shock when, at 0600 in the morning of the morning of which we speak of which, I was awakened by a voice that boomed the message, "Holy cow, it's raining!"

I was bent over a desk piled high with papers and reports, time cards and spreadsheets, when the voice jolted me back to the Ordinary World. I leaped to my feet and opened my...that is, tried to focus my bleary eyes. They were very bleary from all the paperwork, don't you see.

I noticed right away that it was dark, yet the darkness wasn't totally dark. It seemed to be mixed with twinkles of distant light. What was going on around here? I hit the button that activated Data Control's Emergency Intercom System.

"Houston? This is Faded Bloomers. We're picking up twinkles of light and might have had a near-miss with a starfish. Send Drover to the office at once to pick up his report card, over!"

HOLY COW
it's
RAINING!

The radio crackled as I waited for a reply. At last it came. "Hairy okra in the tamale pudding... whippersnapper fiddle faddle and bonking bananas."

"Houston? Come back on that. What are we supposed to do with all the bananas? Over."

"Sniggle bop lollipop."

"Roger that. Re-compute the landing data and pass the biscuits, over."

In the eerie darkness, I heard...I thought I heard...*someone yawn*. Was that possible? I mean, we were on space mission, so how...but then someone said, "Boy, I wish I had a biscuit."

I leaned into the mike. "Houston? We've got a Code Red up here, repeat, CODE RED! We've encountered a squadron of Biscuit Eaters. They're armed with forks and spoons. Request permission to request permission, and hurry! Over."

The silence of deep space throbbed, then...the voice again. "Who are you talking to?"

"Houston, they seem to be fluent in Bow-Wow and want to talk. How do we deal with this? Over."

"Oh, I get it. You're talking in your sleep. You know, I think it's started to rain."

"Houston, they've started a train. They're trying to hijack a train!"

"Hank, wake up."

Somehow they had gotten my name and were trying to hijack a whole trainload of bananas! Unless Houston sent us procedures on this...

Huh?

Wait, hold everything. I blinked my eyes and

glanced around. Sniffatory Sensors kicked in and we began receiving a burst of familiar smells, suggesting...suggesting that we were not in a NASA spacecraft fifty miles above the earth, but rather...

Okay, in Slim Chance's living room. Ha ha. In fact, Slim seemed to be coming down the hallway. He walked to the front door, opened it, and stepped out on the porch. Then I heard his voice. "By grabs, it is raining!"

I glanced around the gloom. "Drover, are you there?"

"Where?"

"Wherever you are."

"Yep, I'm wherever I am. Hi."

"Hi. Do you know anything about a train?"

"Well, they say, 'Choo-choo.'"

"I'm aware of that, but did you see one?"

"No, I said it's starting to *rain*. Slim said so too."

"Why is everyone talking about rain?"

"'Cause it's raining, I guess."

"Outside?"

"It always rains outside."

"Don't get smart with me, soldier. I'm just trying to..."

Okay, let's slow down and see if we can sort this out. A neutral observer, such as yourself, might have thought that you were listening in on a conversation between Mission Control and an orbiting spacecraft. And you might have thought that the space agency had finally come to its senses and recruited a top-of-the-line, blue-ribbon cowdog for its space program.

I'm sorry to disappoint you. What you heard was actually Drover and me, carrying on a fairly incoherent conversation in Slim's living room.

To be perfectly honest, I must have fallen asleep. On guard duty. On my ranch. And so did my assistant.

Remember our discussion about how the Security Division had been working brutal hours, day and night? Well, it had finally caught up with me and I had slipped into a doze, dragged down by all the cares and worries of protecting my people, my ranch, my yard, my porch, and all the little children.

After a while, it adds up and we crash. A dog is only a dog.

It happens to dogs every day all over the world. It happens very seldom around here, but by George, once in a while, it happens. A dog is only...I've already said that. It's nothing to be proud of, is the point, and I guess you've noticed that I'm embarrassed about this.

It really hurts, and I won't try to hide behind a bunch of lame excuses. Drover and I had slacked our duties and had slept through the most dangerous part of the night. It was disgraceful, against Ranch Regulations, and I was so ashamed, I made a mental note to give Drover ten Chicken Marks.

I hate being hard on the men, but this business of sleeping on the job had to stop.

Anyway, we can call off the Code Red. Sometimes the mind plays tricks.

There, I've said it, and now you know a dark secret that I wasn't anxious to share. I hope you will keep your trap shut and not spread it around. Thanks.

Where were we? Oh yes, the bananas. We'd just gotten a report that someone had hijacked a whole trainload of...wait, that was a bogus report, skip it. We knew nothing about trains or bananas.

Let's get on with this. I pried my assistant out of bed and we rushed to the porch to get a closer look at this rare event. See, that year in the Texas Panhandle, rain was a very big deal.

Now we're cooking.

CHAPTER TWO

Drover Robs a Train

S orry for all the confusion. It won't happen again, not on my watch.

Show me a dog that sleeps his life away and I'll show you a mutt that never solves a case.

Okay, Drover and I rushed to the screen door, assuming that Slim would be holding it open for us. Hey, dogs want to see rain just as much as people do, right? But the door was closed, so I gave it a shove with my...BONK...with my nose, but that didn't work out so well. Ouch.

Behind me, Drover said, "It's closed."

"No kidding? I hardly noticed—as I bashed my nose into it. Why don't you try to be helpful and nose it open yourself?"

"With my nose?"

I melted him with a glare. "Do you think you can nose it open with your ear?"

"I never thought about that."

"Well, think about it. It's impossible to nose open a door with anything but a nose."

"How come?"

"Because...because that's just the way things work in the Real World. Have you ever thought of joining the Real World?"

"Oh, I'm kind of busy right now."

"Yes, I saw how busy you were—sleeping on the job and slurping your duty."

"You mean shirking?"

"What?"

"You said I was slurping my duty, but I think you meant shirking."

I could feel my temper rising. "I said you were slurping on the job and sleeping your duty! I can't make it any plainer than that. Ten Chicken Marks for slurping your duty."

"Oh drat."

"Now open the nose with your door."

"Yeah, but by doze is stobbed ubb."

"Does anyone care if your doze is stobbed ub?"

"I guess not."

"Nobody cares, so scratch on the screen with your foot."

"Well, this old leg's been giving me fits."

"Never mind, get out of the way."

I shoved him aside, faced the door, and began warming up the muscles in my enormous shoulders. This obstinate door was blocking our path to the porch and our Nose-Opening Procedures had failed. Slim needed to be informed that we were trapped inside the house, and I had no choice but to do Paw Scrapes on the screen.

I placed my right front paw on the screen, hit the Activate Claws button, and pulled my foot downward in a downward direction.

Skritch!

That got his attention. "Hey, meathead, quit scratching my screen door!"

Well, open it!

"We ain't living in a boxcar."

I never said we were living in a boxcar.

"If you shred up my screen, guess who has to replace it. Me."

Boy, he sure gets bent out of shape over nothing.

"It wouldn't hurt if you learned a few manners."

Sigh.

"I guess you want out."

Of course I wanted out! Why else would a dog scratch the screen?

At last, he appeared. Through the screen and in the gloom of morning, he looked...well, awful, what else can you say? Naked except for a pair of boxer shorts, bony, as pale as mayonnaise, and a buzzard's nest of hair on top of his head.

Just for a moment, he reminded me of...well, Frankincense, the famous monster. Deep in my heart, I knew that he couldn't possibly...on the other hand...yipes, he sure looked like Frankincense, and I mean down to the last grizzly detail!

You know, one of the things we learn in Security Work is that the world can be a very strange place, and we have to force ourselves to exercise caution. I mean, weird things happen all the time, and just because I thought this guy was Slim Chance didn't mean...

Just to be on the safe side, I took a step backward and fired off a bark. It drew a rapid response.

"Dry up, will you?"

Okay, it was Slim. Whew.

He jerked open the door. "House-wrecker."

I squirted through the gap and wasn't surprised when he kicked me with his bare foot. It didn't hurt, but...well, it seemed undignified. What kind of world are we living in when the

Head of Ranch Security gets a kick in the pants for wanting to share Porch Time with his master? It seemed a sad state of affairs.

Oh, and by the way, Drover managed to slither outside without getting kicked. I don't know how he always...oh well.

I sat down on the edge of the porch, as far away from Mister Grump as I could get. I turned my back on him too. He didn't deserve the companionship of a dog, and I wasn't sure we would ever be friends again.

The rain made a steady sizzle on the tin roof,

and my goodness, the air smelled wonderful—fresh, damp, heavy with the aroma of sagebrush and old leaves and new grass that was trying to green up. During a drought, we forget how good the world can smell when it gets a drink.

We sat on the porch for a while, listening to the soft rain and breathing in the delicious air and watching daylight creep over the eastern sky. Drover was sitting nearby, and I noticed that he wore a silly grin on his mouth.

"What are you grinning about?"

"Me? Oh, nothing much."

"I'm sure that's true, but when someone grins on this ranch, I need to know what's going on."

"Well, I had a crazy dream."

"Oh? Then we needn't waste any more time. I'm not interested in your dreams."

"Thanks. I dreamed I was a famous astronaut, flying through space in a saddle-up."

"In a saddle-up?"

"Yeah, one of those things they launch into space."

I heaved a sigh. "Drover, get it right. If you were flying through space, it was in a *satellite*, which has nothing to do with a saddle."

"They sound the same."

"They're not the same."

"Well, mine had a saddle."

"Okay, your satellite had a saddle, and I have no interest in hearing the rest of your dream."

He gave me a sly grin. "I haven't gotten to the good part. I robbed a train."

"You robbed a train? In outer space?"

"Yeah, it was a whole train-load of bananas!"

I stared into the vast emptiness of his gaze. "I can't believe we're talking about this. In the first place, it's ridiculous. If someone were listening to this conversation, he'd think we're just a couple of goofballs. In the second place, that wasn't your dream, it was MINE!"

"Gosh, you mean..."

"Stop butting into my dreams! Find your own."

"Hee hee hee."

"And don't giggle in the miggle of my lecture!"

"If that was your dream, *you were asleep*! Hee hee. I caught you!"

Huh?

I paced to the edge of the porch and gazed off into the distance. Many thoughts tramped across the parade ground of my mind. "Drover, in your own sneaking, slithering way, you've exposed a shameful truth about the Security Division. We both slept when we should have been guarding the house. Let's try to put it behind us. Agreed?"

"Okay, but what about my Chicken Marks?"

I marched back to him and laid a paw upon his shoulder. "I'll handle that. Nobody will ever know. Now, let's shape up and try to do better."

Pretty touching, huh? You bet. Our human friends have no idea how hard we strive to be good dogs. Sometimes we fail, but we're never content with failure. We just have to pick ourselves up and march onward, knowing that... well, if we mess up again, we won't tell anyone.

The somber mood of this occasion was suddenly shattered by Slim's voice. "The dadgum rain quit!"

I had been so distracted by departmental business, I hadn't noticed this crucial detail. I lifted Earatory Scanners and sure enough, our instruments confirmed that *the rain had stopped.*

A shiver passed through my biver...through my body, let us say. Why the shiver? Because I knew that Slim would be mad or half-mad for the rest of the day, and the job of cheering him up would fall squarely on us—his dogs.

CHAPTER THREE

Bachelor Breakfast

Okay, Slim had been sitting in a chair on the porch, and suddenly sprang out of the chair. That was pretty remarkable, because the man wasn't famous for springing around in the early morning hours, but he sprang out of his chair and headed for the rain gauge, which was nailed to the top of a gate post.

Wait. Should the word be "sprang" or "sprung?" You know me, I want to get it right. Why? The kids. We don't want them going around, talking like a bunch of peanut-crunching chimpanzees. Here, let's take a closer look at this:

Tic, tack, toe.
Rick, rack, roe.
Ting, tang, tongue.

Spring, sprang, sprung.

And there's our answer. "Slim **sprung** out of his chair." Wow, is this amazing or what? Your ordinary mutts know nothing about this stuff, and we're talking about your town dogs, your poodles and your Chihuahuas. They're pampered and lazy, and they never give a thought to the future of this nation. If the kids start talking like monkeys, they don't care.

You know who cares? Cowdogs. Heads of Ranch Security. ME.

Now...where were we? Hmm. Bananas? Yes. When monkeys aren't crunching peanuts and leaving shells all over the place, they're consuming large quantities of bananas and speaking gibberish. This nation will never prosper as long as...

Wait. We were on the porch, right? And Slim Chance had sprung out of his chair and was walking barefoot toward the rain gauge, right? Now we're on it.

You know, dogs see a lot of things we can't talk about. Imagine this scene. In day's first light, a full-grown, half-naked cowboy-scarecrow was walking barefoot across an expanse of mud, in an area that normal people would describe as "the yard." Ha. See, most of the grass in Slim's so-called yard had perished in the drought, leaving a few brave stalks of ragweed that were still clinging to life. Mostly, the "yard" was pure dirt, only now it had turned into mud.

The guy was walking barefooted through the MUD, on his way to the rain gauge, and he didn't seem to care that mud was oozing up between his toes. I'm not kidding. Even on the porch, I could see it.

He made it to the gate and snatched the glass tube out of the rain gauge holder. He brought the tube close to his face and glared at it. "Twenty-five hundredths and a spider!" He turned a flaming pair of eyes toward the sky and shook his fist. "Sissy clouds! We need five inches and you give us twenty-five hundredths!"

And then...this was hard to believe...he drew back his arm and threw the rain gauge as far as he could throw it, which was pretty far. It sailed across the gravel drive and shattered against the south side of the saddle shed.

A ghoulish smile leaped across his mouth and he yelled, "There, by grabs, see how you like that!"

Amazing.

He stomped back to the porch and threw himself into his chair. Hard. He seemed to be expressing his anger by throwing his body into the chair, don't you see, and never suspected that it would tip over backwards. Guess what? It did.

His muddy bare feet shot up from the floor and arched above his head, and he and the chair went crashing into the wall.

What can you say?

I turned my gaze away from him and pretended that I didn't notice. As I've said, we dogs have stories that must be locked away in the safety deposit box of our heart—stories we can't share with anyone, and stories that nobody would believe anyway.

As Slim was picking himself off the floor, I went to Taps of Sympathy on the tail section and switched on a facial expression that said, "I saw nothing. Honest."

He set the chair back where it belonged, brushed a briar patch of hair out of his eyes, heaved a sigh, and sat down, this time in a civilized manner. He threw one leg over the opposite knee and stared at his foot, which was caked with mud.

A heavy silence fell upon us, then he spoke. "A man gets a little crazy in a drought."

Oh? I had hardly noticed.

"When we need a good soaking rain and get a stinking little shower...well, it hurts, pooch. You can understand that."

Right, exactly, and I was doing my best to

share his pain.

"My feet got muddy."

Well...yes. Duh. When you walk barefoot through mud, your feet get muddy.

"Hank, I've got an idea on how we can fix that."

Oh brother. I knew this was coming.

"Come here." I went. "Lie down and hold still."

I did as I was told. I lay there like a door mat, whilst he wiped his muddy feet on the hair of my back and ribs, and cleaned his toes with the flap of my left ear. Drover watched from the other side of the porch, out of harm's way, and GRINNED.

"There! Good dog. Anybody who says you're worthless just don't know the full story." He yawned and stretched. "I wonder what we could rustle up for breakfast." He pushed himself out of the chair and looked down at me. "How'd you get so muddy?"

He thinks he's funny.

He brushed some of the mud off my coat. "I guess you can come in, and I might even share my breakfast. How does that sound?"

Breakfast? I was no pushover, but...well, a good breakfast can heal a lot of wounds.

I followed him into the house, and I'm proud to report that Drover wasn't invited. Good. He didn't deserve to be part of our Inner Circle. Don't forget that he had grinned while I was being used as a foot-scraper. That would go into his record—grinning at the misfortunes of a superior officer.

I followed Slim into the kitchen—a loyal dog

preparing to share Precious Breakfast Moments with his cowboy companion. He gave me a wink. "How 'bout some bacon and eggs?"

Slurp. Perfect. Yes!

He opened the ice box door, bent over, and looked inside. "Well, I see that we're out of bacon, but that'll work, 'cause we're out of eggs too."

Oh brother.

He reached inside. "Wait. Lookie here, pooch, some left-over boiled chicken gizzards."

Chicken gizzards! For breakfast?

He brought out a plastic bread bag containing three pounds of gizzards that he had boiled up who-knows-when. He dumped them out on a paper plate. I guess that was his idea of "food presentation," dumping a mess of cold grayish-green chicken gizzards onto a paper plate.

Have you ever looked at a bunch of boiled gizzards in the morning? Let me tell you something, it's shocking. A cold gizzard reminds you of something that came out of a dead chicken, and you have to wonder...what kind of man eats those things for breakfast? And why?

I mean, this is the modern age and we have grocery stores. Even Twitchell has one. They sell things like bacon and eggs, steak and pork chops. All you have to do is drive into town and do a little shopping.

Oh well. A dog can't spend his life grieving over all the bacon and eggs that didn't show up. Remember the Wise Old Saying? "There will be days when Life offers nothing but cold chicken gizzards for breakfast." That's a great Wise Old Saying, and it hits Truth right between the nose.

But to be fair about it, I had to admit that while the gizzards didn't look very appetizing, they smelled pretty...sniff, sniff...what was that smell? Gag!

Even Slim noticed, and he had the nose of a brick. His eyes widened and his lip curled. "Good honk, I think they've started to decompose."

Decompose! What kind of zoo was this?

He rushed to the back door and threw them outside. On his way back, he looked at me and said, "Don't eat 'em, pooch. They're past their prime."

I had never been so insulted. Did I look dumb enough to eat a pile of decomposing chicken gizzards? Let me address that question in two stages.

Stage One: I most certainly was NOT dumb enough to eat a pile of crawly decomposing chicken gizzards that smelled so gruesome, he'd pitched them out into the back yard. What kind of moron...

Stage Two: On the other hand, a dog must

keep his options open. Until we actually ran tests, we wouldn't know whether they had become toxic or were just, well, passing through a Cheesy Phase.

See, cheese smells cheesy because it's *aged*, and that's crucial to this whole discussion about our food supply. Many types of food improve during the Aging Process, don't you know, and we would have to suspend judgment on the material in the back yard until we, uh, received an update on the Breakfast Situation.

It's pretty amazing that a dog would pay such close attention to diet and nutrition, isn't it? You bet. Your ordinary run of mutts never give it a thought. They'll eat anything—scraps, garbage, and the factory-made sawdust products that come in a fifty-pound sack and are passed off as "dog food."

On this outfit, we make a serious study of what we put into our mouths. We never forget that what we eat is who we are. Food feeds the mind, and the mind of a dog is an awesome thing.

Now, where were we? I have no idea. Tell you what, let's erase the blackboard, change chapters, get ourselves organized, and regroup on the other side.

I hope you enjoyed our Unit on Nutrition.

CHAPTER FOUR

Bad News
on the Radio

Oh yes, breakfast. Slim was tramping around
the kitchen in his underwear, and I was
waiting for some hints on what he might offer for
breakfast.

It wasn't looking good. He was out of bacon
and eggs. He had thrown parts of a dead chicken
out the back door. Pancakes and waffles weren't
even a possibility because he would never make
anything that required measuring or stirring,
thought, preparation, or patience.

Toast? How about some toast with Sally
May's wild plum jelly? There wasn't much he
could do to mess up a piece of toast.

Nope, toast was out too. The half-loaf of bread
he found in the cabinet was sprouting hairy

green mold. You know what he said? "You wouldn't think that mold could grow in a drought, would you? I guess I need to do an inventory once in a while."

Inventory. Oh brother.

He held the package of bread above his head, bent his knees, and sent a nice, soft, arching shot toward the trash can on the other side of the room. It was a long shot, and I wouldn't have bet that he could make it...plunk...but he did.

He was proud of himself and flashed a grin. "That was a three-pointer, pooch. You know, the Celtics tried to draft me right out of the eighth grade, but I was too serious about my studies to go off and get famous."

I had no idea what he was talking about, but it sounded like a windy tale.

He opened a cabinet door and squinted at a collection of canned goods. "How 'bout some green beans?"

I dropped my gaze to the floor. No.

"How 'bout stewed dummaters?"

Dogs don't eat tomatoes.

He rummaged around some more. "Here we go! I've got fifteen cans of mackerel. How does that sound?"

Was he serious? Dead fish for breakfast? NO!

He gave me an ugly scowl. "Listen, dog, you ain't Mrs. Vanderbilt's toy schnauzer. Sometimes we have to cowboy-up and live off the land." He heaved a sigh. "Okay, canned mackerel don't sound so great to me either. Let's skip breakfast and listen to some happy music."

He switched on an old radio he kept on the counter and we heard a news report. He listened for about thirty seconds, made a sour face, and... well, began talking to the radio.

"Listen, you. I'm living in the middle of a drought and that's all the bad news I can stand." He twisted the dial to another station, and got another blast of breaking news. I could see that he was getting mad. "You hammerheads report all the bad news you can drag up. You want to give me a headache so you can sell me some aspirin. Well, I don't need any aspirin." He looked down at me. "If they can't find any good news, why don't they just shut up and go find an honest job?"

I agreed. In fact, I barked at the radio, just to let 'em know that, by George, we dogs didn't want any more of their dreary news. Or their aspens.

There! Slim and I had struck a blow for dogs and cowboys all across the globe.

Wearing a ferocious scowl, Slim turned the

dial from station to station, until he finally found some soft, soothing music. Whew, just in time to save us from...I don't know what he might have done if this had gone on another minute, probably something crazy. Maybe some soothing music would pull his brink back from the edge of the periphery.

But you know what? The song turned out to be not as soothing as you might have expected. You want to hear it?

Bad News

Bad news. Worse news.
Ca-tas-tro-phe.
Scandals. Wrecks. Explosions.
Live on teevee.

Gold is down. So's the Pound.
Investments are in the tank.
Hide your cash beneath the mattress.
Chances are, they'll close the bank.

Angry mobs are throwing garbage at
   their leaders,
And a hurricane destroyed a beach.
Infectious germs are getting stronger by

the minute,
And the president will give another speech.

Sin, decay, and corruption.
Too far advanced to reverse.
We hope you have a splendid afternoon
Because tomorrow very likely will be worse.
It will be worse.
Ba-a-a-ad News.

When the song ended, we heard the announcer's voice. "There you are, folks, 'Bad News,' the latest smash hit from the Bathtub Choral Society. Give us a call and let us know what you think of it."

My eyes were locked on Slim. I held my breath and waited for what would happen next. I couldn't even imagine. He stood as silent as a pillar of salt, twirling a strand of hair around his finger. His eyes were pinched and his mouth had become as thin as barbed wire.

At last he spoke—again, to the radio. "Okay, buddy, here's what I think." He took a grip on the power cord and jerked the plug out of the socket. "Dry up!" He dusted his hands together and gave me a grin. "They ain't going to ruin my day. I can do that all by myself. What do you think of that, pooch?"

Well, it was...actually, it struck me as a little weird, I mean, who else does stuff like that? But it seemed to have a calming effect on his Inner Bean, and that was important. We wanted him to start the day with a good attitude in his Inner Bean.

Wait. Inner Bean. Remember that can of green beans? Was this some kind of clue that might send the case...never mind, skip it.

He took a big stretch and glanced around the kitchen. "Well, we got breakfast out of the way, and I probably ought to put on some clothes, before we go out and do heroic things."

Right. He looked ridiculous in his underwear.

He started toward the hallway. Suddenly I noticed a flashing light on the control panel of my mind: "STARVING!"

I streaked toward the back door and configured my entire body into an arrow that was pointing outside. Slim noticed. He stopped and turned around. "You need to answer the Call of the Wild?"

Yes, exactly, the Call of the Wild.

He slouched to the door and pushed it open. "I hope everything comes out all right. See you later."

Ay ay, sir!

I darted outside and headed straight for... wait, hold everything. We've encountered a gap in the story, no kidding. Something must have gone haywire in Data Control. You know how it is. Wires get crossed, a circuit breaker blows, happens all the time, no big deal. Anyway, we've lost a short segment of the story.

Don't worry about the part you're missing. Almost nothing happened. Five minutes later, the Starving Light had quit blinking, and I found myself sitting on the porch, waiting for Slim to begin the day's work. Heh heh.

Drover was there, of course. It appeared that he hadn't moved an inch, and he looked kind of downcast. "What's wrong with you?"

"I didn't get any breakfast."

"Yes, well, you didn't deserve any breakfast, so it all worked out."

"Did he fix bacon and eggs?"

"Yes. No. It's none of your business. All you need to know is that a solution was found."

"That's a funny way to put it. Was it breakfast or a solution?"

"It was both, but more of a solution than a breakfast."

"What does that mean?"

"It means that sometimes we have to make compromises."

"I don't get it."

"Drover, you don't get half of what goes on in

your shriveled little world, and you don't need to get it. Life will go right on without your help."

"Yeah, I try to be helpful."

I glared down into his face. "When did you ever try to be helpful?"

"That day...oh, five years ago, but I don't remember what I did. Do you smell cheese?"

"What?"

"I smell cheese...bad cheese. Yuck! You don't smell it?"

I ran a Sniffatory Analysis. "I don't smell anything unusual. Maybe you need a bath."

He made a sour face, then his gaze drifted upward toward the sky. "I'll be derned. Lookie there. Buzzards."

I lifted my eyes and saw them. "Yes, two of them. They're circling."

"Oh my gosh, they're coming here!"

"Don't be absurd. Why would buzzards come here?" We continued to watch the big black birds, wheeling through the air in circles that seemed... hmm, to be bringing them in our direction. "You know what? I think they're coming here."

"I knew it! Let's hide!"

"Hide from what? Buzzards are harmless."

"Yeah, but they're ugly and creepy, and all they ever do is eat things that are dead."

"Well, since we're not dead, we have nothing to fear. And you know what else?"

"What else?"

"We know those buzzards, Wallace and Junior."

Drover was fretting. "I don't know any buzzards, and if I did, I wouldn't tell anyone. I've got nothing to say to a buzzard and I'm out of here!"

He went streaking around the south side of the house.

Drover had responded in a chicken-hearted manner, but he had raised a couple of good points. First, buzzards are ugly and creepy, and second, when they show up, what do you talk about?

I was fixing to find out, because at that very moment, while the dust from Drover's escape still hung in the air, Wallace and Junior crash-landed in the front yard.

Don't leave. You'll want to hear this.

CHAPTER FIVE

Buzzards Arrive

Buzzards are graceful when they're floating around in the air. If you didn't know they were buzzards, you might even say they were beautiful. They're also fairly graceful perched in a tree or on the edge of a caprock. I mean, they have a pretty impressive profile up there, and you might even mistake one for an eagle.

But they're not graceful on the ground. Buzzards weren't designed to do anything you can do with a good set of legs, such as walk, run, jump, or play. They're not even very good at coming in for a landing.

Wallace came in first. Ten feet off the ground, he spread out his wings and began reducing his speed. I could hear him talking to himself.

"Landing gear down! Flaps down! Beacon on! Speed ten knots! Altitude nine foot six inches! Y'all better get out of the way, we're coming in a little hot!"

He came in "a little hot," all right, and his skinny legs took quite a jolt. Wham! He bounced twice, nosed over and did a forward roll. He came to a stop and pried himself off the ground.

"Junior, cut your speed, runway's full of potholes!"

Junior was making his approach. "O-okay, Pa-a-a, h-h-here I c-c-c-come!"

Wallace whipped his head around and saw me on the porch. "What are you staring at?"

"Oh, I was just watching the show. How long did it take you to learn to do summersaults?"

"Are you making fun?"

"No question about it."

"You know, dog, an honest job would cure a lot of your problems—a job and a piece of duct tape over that smart mouth."

"You're fixing to get creamed."

Wallace puffed himself up to his full height. "Oh yeah? By you and whose army?"

"By your own son."

"Huh?" He snapped his head around, just in time to see what was coming his way: Junior.

"Hey! Pull up, pull up, abort landing! Son, you're a-coming in too…"

BAM! Wallace tried to scramble out of the way, but Junior lit right in the middle of him, and boy, you talk about legs, wings, and feathers! Junior popped him good and they both went rolling.

When old Wallace quit rolling and scrambled to his feet, he was torqued. "What part of ABORT LANDING don't you understand!"

"W-w-w-well…

"It don't mean wreck your daddy!"

"W-w-w-well…"

"If you don't learn how to drive that thing, you're liable to kill off the whole family!"

"S-s-sorry, P-p-pa, b-but y-you were in the w-w-way."

"Me in the way! Son, when there's aircraft on the runway, you can't land! You pull up and go around for another shot. And I'll tell you another thing. Never wreck your daddy in front of a crowd."

"W-w-what c-c-crowd?"

The old man shot a wing-tip in my direction. "Him!"

Junior turned and saw me on the porch, and a pleasant grin spread across his beak. "Oh m-m-my, it's our d-d-doggie f-f-friend, doggie friend. H-h-hi, d-d-d-doggie."

Wallace shook his head. "Junior, don't be giving him that 'hi-doggie' stuff. Nobody in this family has ever made friends with a dog, and we ain't fixing to start now."

"Oh, P-p-a, h-he's okay."

"He ain't okay! Just look at him." They both turned to me. "He's got nothing better to do than sit there like a potted plant and stick his big nose into somebody else's business."

"W-w-well, w-w-we l-landed on h-h-his r-ranch, his ranch."

"Yes sir, and we had a collision that could have killed somebody. Do you know what your doggie friend done? He laughed and ran his big mouth."

"Wh-what did he s-s-s-say?"

"He said...he asked your daddy how long it took him to learn to do summersaults."

Junior giggled. "Hee hee. Oh, th-that's f-f-f-funny!"

"Funny my foot! Son, we might need to send you back to mortuary school and work on your attitude. Sometimes you forget who you are."

"O-o-o-kay, P-pa."

"You ain't a canary."

"O-okay, P-p-pa."

"You're a buzzard, and you need to start acting

like one."

"S-s-sorry."

"Now, get off your duff and let's locate that signal I was a-picking up in the sky."

"M-m-maybe the d-d-doggie could h-h-help."

"Junior, we don't need help from..." Wallace snapped his head around and gave me a glare. "Reckon he'd help? He's kind of a smarty-pants."

"W-w-w-well, I c-c-could a-ask him, ask him."

Wallace shook his head. "You sit tight and take notes. We'll use the A-Team on this deal." Wallace waddled in my direction, and seemed to be forcing a pleasant expression on his face. "Morning."

"Morning."

"Awful dry, ain't it? That little shower we got wouldn't even rust a nail." Silence. Wallace rocked up and down on his toes. "Dog, me and Junior have fallen on hard times in this drought, is what's happened. Our business was off twenty-six percent last month."

"Huh. I would have thought that hard times would be good for the buzzard business."

"Well, you would have thought wrong. I guess it's a good thing you ain't a buzzard." Another awkward silence moved over us. "Here's the deal, dog. Me and Junior was a-flying Recon this morning and picked up a bodacious strong signal, coming from somewhere close to the house."

"Slim's house?"

"Pooch, I don't know who owns the house. Buzzards don't do property law. I'm a-telling you that we picked up a powerful signal, I mean, it lit up the whole screen. It was something dead, it was close to this house, and you ought to be able to smell it, if your nose works at all."

"I have an excellent nose."

He studied me with a level gaze. "Well, I'll have to take your word on that, 'cause, to be honest, it don't look all that great to me."

"What is that supposed to mean?"

"Well, I hadn't planned to blurt it out, heh, but it kindly reminds me of the sharp end of an anvil, and if you don't believe me, just ask my boy. Junior?"

Junior had been listening. "I th-think his n-n-n-nose l-looks pretty g-g-good, Pa-a-a-a."

The old man flinched. "Junior, nobody around here wants to hear what you think about a dog's nose."

"W-w-well, you a-a-asked, asked."

"That was my first mistake, asking the opinion of a kid." Wallace whirled around to me. "You can't trust these kids anymore. Half the time, they can't even find their own feet, but back to the

41

business, me and Junior could sure use a turn in our luck, yes we could." He rolled his gaze up to the sky. "I don't want to load you down with our troubles, pooch, but we ain't had a decent meal in eight days. Just ask Junior."

"F-f-four d-days, P-p-pa."

"Junior, I'm gonna quit taking you out in public if you don't straighten up! I'm a-talking about a *decent* meal. I know we lucked into that bull snake in the road, but don't forget who hogged most of it."

Junior grinned. "Y-yeah, I b-b-beat you to th-that one, hee hee."

Wallace whirled back to me. "You see what I

mean about these kids? They're all pampered, ungrateful brats and they eat like hogs, but the point I'm a-trying to make is, there's something around this house that sure would make a fine meal for a couple of buzzards, and we'd like to find it."

"Wallace, I just figured out what you're talking about."

A crazy grin slithered across his beak. "Yes, yes? Keep a-talking. Junior, stand by, I think we're a-getting close. Go on, dog."

"Could it have been...three pounds of boiled chicken gizzards?"

"Could be, sure could be. Were they kind of ripe?"

"Yes, they were ripe."

The old man's eyes crackled with pure greed. "Three pounds of chicken gizzards! Yes sir, that's bound to be it. Two for me and one for Junior. Perfect. Where they at?"

"The last I saw, they were behind the house."

"Behind the house? Junior, start your motor, we're fixing to move out. Pooch, a good deed will always come back to bless you, yes it will."

"Oh...there's one problem."

His beak dropped open. "Dog, I don't want to hear about a problem, not today, not with business like it's been."

I leaned closer to him. "I ate 'em."

Through the windows of his eyes, I could see rafters falling. "That ain't possible, dogs don't eat that kind of stuff."

"Well, I did, and I can tell you, those were the best aged gizzards I ever ate. You would have loved 'em, only you were a little slow on the draw."

Wallace whipped his gaze around to Junior. "There it is, son. This back-stabbing, two-timing, anvil-nosed mutt-fuzz of a dog has ate us into the poor house!"

Junior shrugged. "Oh d-d-darn."

"Oh darn is right. We got here too late. Didn't I tell you it was time to get off the roost and hunt grub?"

"W-w-well, I th-think y-you were the one wh-who slept l-l-l-l…who stayed in b-b-b-bed, in bed."

"Well, one way or another, we're snookered. We've been robbed by your so-called doggie friend." He whirled back to me. "Some friend you turned out to be! I'm half a mind to beat the stuffings out of you, right here and now. Junior, hold me back, son, or I'm liable to clean his plow!"

Junior grinned and shook his head. "P-pa, l-let's get b-b-back to w-w-work."

Wallace took a couple of backward steps, but

continued glaring spears and daggers at me. "You lucked out this time, dog. Junior won't let me fight any more, else I'd thrash your hide, but paybacks are headed your way, yes they are, and do you know how I know?"

"No, I don't know how you know."

He narrowed his eyes to wicked slits and dropped his voice to a croak. "What shows up on Buzzard Radar wasn't meant for a dog to eat. Remember that, puppy."

"I'll do that, Wallace, and thanks for everything. This has been fun, now scram."

"Who's telling me to scram?"

I stepped off the porch and gave him my Special Train Horns Bark right in the face. BWONK! "Me!"

He staggered backward. "Junior, are you gonna just sit there and let that dog bark in your daddy's face?" He whipped his head around to me. "Junior knows karotto and it wouldn't take him three seconds to chop your neck off!"

Junior rolled his eyes. "P-p-pa, c-c-come on. L-let's g-g-get airborne."

Wallace leveled a wing at me. "Junior's going to let you off easy this time, puppy dog, but if it ever happens again, I can't guarantee that I can hold him back."

"P-pa, j-j-just h-h-hush!"

"Okay, fine, I'll hush. Flaps down, full power, and I get first dibs on whatever we find!"

Wallace hopped several steps, flapped his big wings, and rose into the sky. Junior lingered for a moment, gave me a shy grin, and shrugged. "H-h-he g-g-gets s-s-silly s-s-sometimes."

"We all have kinfolks, Junior. Good luck with the grub."

And with that, they were gone and out of my borp...excuse me, out of my life.

CHAPTER SIX

Food Freedom

When the buzzards had gone, peace and tranquittery returned to my ranch, and I went looking for the King of Slackers. Drover. I found him huddled behind the only piece of landscaping in Slim's yard, a native plant that probably could have survived on Mars.

It was one of those plants with the long sharp-pointed leaves. You probably don't know this, but they go by four names: yucca, bear grass, Spanish dagger, and I don't remember the other one.

And who cares? What makes a yucca plant think it deserves four names anyway? It might deserve one name, just barely, because all it ever does around here is poke dogs in the side with its daggery leaves, and they hurt. This ranch would

47

get along just fine if all the whatchamacallits packed up and left.

Okay, maybe they do one thing that's kind of nice. When we get moisture in the spring, they spend the whole month of May putting out big white blooms from a stalk that grows in the center of the plant, and I have to admit that the Flowering of the Yuccas is pretty impressive. For two or three weeks, they light up the prairie landscape, tall white blossoms everywhere.

I'll tell you one more thing about those yuccas, then we have to rush back to the story. Cows love to eat the blossoms. If you're driving cattle across country, they'll race from one plant to the other, gobbling the flowers. The cowboys have to yell and swing their ropes to get 'em to move along— the cows, that is, not the flowers. The flowers don't move.

Sometimes our ranch executives show good sense and roll out their Secret Weapon. They let ME go to work, chewing their hocks and heels. Heh. That's a blast, gnawing on the ankles of an old rip that has lost her mind over a feast of yucca salad. It's easy money...unless they kick, of course, and that can be pretty shocking. I mean, your average thousand-pound cow can deliver a blow and airmail your average cowdog quite a distance.

Anyway, that's today's Unit on Prairie Wildlife. I hope you enjoyed it and maybe even learned something. It's kind of impressive that a dog would know all that stuff, isn't it? You bet.

Wait! I just remembered the fourth name for that plant: soapweed. There we go, I knew it would come to me, and now you're wondering, "How come they call it soapweed?" Great question, but I don't know the answer.

Where were we? Boy, a dog sure can get borp... excuse me, distracted, and you know, that brings another subject to mind. Remember those gizzards that Slim pitched out the back door? Well, I never actually came right out and told you what happened to them, but you might have picked up a few clues in my conversation with Wallace.

In case you missed the clues, here's the scoop. I ate 'em. Hee hee! Yes sir, when Slimbo let me out to "answer the Call of the Wild," I answered the Call of the Wild Chicken Gizzards—streaked right to 'em, crunched 'em up, and wolfed 'em down, and we're talking about wolfing like a wolf.

I had to do it fast, don't you know, because, well, Slim had told me not to eat them, and I sure didn't want to appear disobedient while he was watching. When you face a heavy moral decision and find that your conscience demands that you disobey an order, you should do it when the people have gone back inside the house.

See, everyone is happier that way. The dog is able to follow his conscience, and our people don't need to know. As I've pointed out before, one of the toughest parts of a dog's job is figuring out which of their instructions we should ignore.

Hey, no dog can follow their instructions all the time, and if we tried, we'd end up as...I don't know, poodles or stuffed animals. We would surrender our Deeper Dogness to well-intentioned friends who—pay close attention to this—to well-intentioned friends WHO HAVE NEVER BEEN A DOG.

You hadn't thought of that, had you? Well, think about it. Those amongst us who have never been a dog shouldn't be telling real dogs how to live their lives. I mean, they're good people, don't get me wrong, and in some ways, they're pretty smart, but they have never lived life as a dog.

They just don't understand.

Which takes us right back to the Case of the Chicken Gizzards. Slim was being kind and sincere when he told me not to eat the material, but he was applying his own limited experience as a bachelor cowboy to my life as a dog.

I won't deny that he'd had a long and sad history with tainted food in his ice box. I mean, I'd been there on several occasions when he'd been knocked flat by something called "Cinderella," also know as "food poisoning."

Salmonella, I guess it should be.

Remember his famous Two Week Spaghetti? Ha! He made this huge pot of spaghetti, ate a little dab every night, added more spaghetti, kept putting it back in the ice box, and repeated the drill for two weeks. It was a great idea that brought tragic consequences: he got Cinderella. So nobody could blame him for being gun-shy about stuff in the ice box that acquired green mold and a cheesy smell.

What Slim didn't know was that when he pitched that spaghetti out the back door, I ate every bite of it and had no problems. None. And I scarfed it down in two minutes, not two weeks.

Yes, Slim was a decent, caring man, but he *wasn't a dog*. Not one day in his entire life had he ever been a dog, and what he didn't know about a dog's digestatory processes would have filled a library.

Don't forget the Wise Old Saying: "What's goose for the sauce is duck for the gander." In other words, if you've never been a dog, don't tell dogs how to borp...excuse me, how to be dogs. It's wrong and unnatural.

The simple, scientific fact is that dogs can eat and digest certain food groups that are uneekable to our human friends. We drink muddy water out of creeks, cow tracks, and stock tanks. We eat bacon grease, steak fat, gristle, cartilage, roast beef trimmings, corn cobs, baked potato hulls, and chicken bones. Eating that stuff is not a big deal to a dog.

I have even eaten Sally May's Desert-Dry Corn Bread, which came close to bumping me off, but I survived, and survival is the bottom line.

Finally, let me borp...excuse me, let me address the testimony of Wallace the Buzzard, who claimed that dogs can't handle any food material that shows up on Buzzard Radar. That was nonsense, exactly the kind of rubbish you'd expect to hear from an arrogant, self-serving, small-minded funeral-home crow.

Let me remind this court that Wallace the Buzzard, like Slim Chance, HAD NEVER BEEN A DOG, and was totally unqualified to be an expert witness on what dogs should eat. Your Honor, with that, we rest our case.

I didn't mean to get so worked up, but by George, this is still America, and we dogs must stand up for our right to eat aged chicken gizzards at any hour of the day or night. It's all about Freedom.

So there's our Unit on Food Freedom. You've probably never given much thought to Food Freedom, but now you know that it's a very big deal to us dogs.

Now…where were we? I have no idea. Rabbits? Maybe that was it. Sometimes my thought processes remind me of the rabbits we see in the springtime, hopping around in circles and acting silly. We never know if they're drunk, crazy, or in love…wait, we weren't talking about rabbits.

Drover. There we go. I had gone around to the south side of Slim's shack, where I found the runt hiding behind a yucca bush. He saw me coming. "Oh, hi. Did they leave?"

"The rabbits?"

"No, the buzzards."

"Oh, them. Yes, we talked for a while and I ordered them off the property."

"Oh good. They're creepy. I wouldn't know what to talk about with a couple of creepy buzzards."

I sat down beside him. "It's easier than you might think, son. Your average buzzard has only one note on his horn."

"They have horns?"

"Drover, that was a figure of speech, a clever, imaginative way of saying that buzzards have a one-track mind. All they can talk about is food."

"Gosh, that sounds like us."

"It does NOT sound like us."

"That's what I meant."

"The mind of a dog is deep and borp."

"What?"

"Deep and wide. Expansive. Without limits."

"Do you smell cheese?"

"Do you want to hear the rest of this or not?"

"Sorry. I thought I smelled cheese."

"Well, you're free to smell anything you want, but I was trying to educate you on the subject of buzzards. Now, you can either remain an ignoramus for the rest of your life, or you can learn something."

His gaze lifted to the sky. "You know, I get tired of being an ignoramus."

"Really? Are you being sincere about that?"

"Yeah, it's kind of depressing, being an ignoramus all the time. It makes me wish that I could be a smartoramus."

"Soldier, I'm proud to hear you say that! I think we're making progress, and we've even invented a new word: *smartoramus*."

"Yeah, I made it up."

"Drover, it was a team effort. Never forget that we're all part of a team."

"Yeah, but I made it up all by myself. I'll bet I could make up a song about it too. You want me to try?"

"No, thank you, we're on a tight schedule this morning."

He glanced around. "Doing what?"

"How long is this song of yours?"

"Oh, it's pretty short."

I heaved a sigh. "Okay, let's get it over with." And with that, he performed his latest masterpiece, "Smartoramus."

> I'm tired of being just an ignoramus.
> A smartoramus is what I want to be,
>   (When I grow up),
> I'll have to take a test, I'll do my level best,
> Smart-o-ramus-isation is for me,
>   (When I grow up).

When he had finished the song, he faced me with a wide grin. "What do you think? Pretty good, huh?"

I began pacing, as I often do when my mind is troubled. "Look, I don't want to hurt your

feelings, but...Drover, that was awful! A proper song is supposed to consist of verses followed by a chorus. That thing was nothing but a chorus, repeated four times."

"Well, I couldn't think of any verses."

"It was a tiresome little chorus, looking for a song."

"Yeah, but it came straight from my heart."

"All right, it was a tiresome little chorus that came straight from your heart, which proves that you need bypass surgery."

"I don't get it. What does that mean?"

"Never mind. What were we talking about? Oh yes, buzzards. My point was that they're obsessed with food."

"Yeah, and all they eat is garbage. What were they doing here?"

"As a matter of fact, they were looking for food. Their radar picked up three pounds of chicken gizzards that Slim chunked out the back door."

"They ate 'em?"

There was a long moment of silence. "Not exactly."

His eyes grew wide. "You didn't eat 'em, did you?" My sly grin must have given the answer. He gasped. "You did? Oh my gosh, what if you get sick?"

"I won't get sick. Dogs who are careful, thorough, and disciplined in their eating don't get borp."

Drover sniffed the air. "There's that cheese again. You don't smell it?"

"No, and we're out of time for questions. Slim just walked out the front door and it's time to go to work. Let's move out."

We raced around to the front of the house, just as our cowboy pal stepped off the porch. He had put on some clothes and looked much better now, wearing something besides his drawers, and we were ready to launch ourselves into a new adventure that involved...

I almost said "a mountain lion," but it's too soon to go public with that. Maybe it will come up later and maybe it won't. To find out for sure, you'll have to keep reading.

If you thought I said "mountain lion," keep it to yourself, okay? Thanks.

CHAPTER SEVEN

A Gizzardly Problem

By the time Slim reached the pickup door, I was already there, poised to leap into the cab. He noticed that I was quivering with anstickipation. "You think you deserve to ride up in First Class?"

Well…yes, of course. Important dogs always ride in the cab. Ordinary mutts can ride in the back with fence posts and sacks of feed.

"I hope you understand what an honor it is to ride up front with me."

Could we get on with this?

He reached for the door handle and…bonk… what a dirty trick! You know what he did? He opened the door just a crack, see, knowing that I would launch myself into the cab, and, naturally, I banged my nose against the door and fell into a heap on the ground.

"Not so fast, pooch. I want to make double-sure that you're grateful and humble and proud to be riding around in a pickup with me."

Oh brother. All right, I was honored.

At last, he swung open the door, but this time, I just sat there, waiting to see if he was going to pull any more tricks. To be honest, I was having second thoughts about riding in the cab with him.

He shrugged. "Fine. You can ride in the back."

Huh?

As I've said before, someone on this outfit has to show some maturity. If the dogs don't do it, who or whom does that leave? Nobody. I flew inside the cab and took my usual place of honor on the shotgun-side, next to the window.

Drover entered the pickup in his usual manner, grunting and clawing his way onto the seat. He puts no style into the Ordinary Events of Life. He just slops through them, but at last, he managed to climb inside and took his spot in the middle of the seat. Slim started the pickup and off we went to new adventures on the ranch.

Once we were moving, Drover said, "How come you never let me ride Shotgun?"

"Because you lack the proper training, and besides, you don't even own a shotgun."

"Yeah, but you don't either."

"Exactly my point. Neither of us owns a shotgun, but I didn't own one long before you didn't. That's a huge difference."

"Yeah, but it's no fair. I feel so unequal, sitting in the middle all the time."

"Wait. You feel 'unequal'? What number are you feeling?" He gave me a blank look. "A number, Drover. If you talk about something being equal to something else, that's a Numbers Situation."

"Oh. Well, let me think." He rolled his eyes around. "Three?"

"Ah! There's your problem. See, you forgot to carry the one over to the left-hand column. You should be feeling thirteen, not three."

He stared at me. "No fooling?"

"Absolutely. You just added wrong."

He blinked his eyes. "I'll be derned. So I'm not as unequal as I thought?"

"Exactly. When we add wrong, nothing adds up."

A smile lifted the limp rope of his mouth. "You know, I think that helped."

I whopped him on the back. "Good, good. Fundamentals, son, it all comes down to bupp."

"What?"

"I said, it all comes down to cheese. Do you notice an odd smell?"

"Yeah, but it's worse than cheese. I hope you're not…"

"Never mind, sorry I bought it up."

I returned to my spot on the Shotgun side and thrust my nose out the window. All at once the air inside the cab seemed stale and stuffy, and I found myself overwhelmed by thoughts of… CHEESE.

You know, some kinds of cheese are pleasant to smell, but others really stink. They remind us of something we might feed to a buzzard, and that wasn't the kind of …

I would NOT give any more thought to cheese or food. There's a time to think about food and a time to think about…well, flowers and bees and butterflies. A disciplined mind can always…

Uh oh. Something was stirring in the depths of my deeps. I stole a quick glance at Slim. His mind was far away and he had no inkling of what kind of disaster might be lurking in our future. Did I dare intrude into the carnival of his mind and alert him to the dangers we were facing?

Yes. This was getting serious and he needed to be warned that…well, that the interior of his pickup was in danger of getting spray-painted the color of used gizzards. The man had no idea what we were facing here.

I swiveled around to the left and fired off three blasts of Alert and Alarm Barking, right over the top of Drover's head. I had a feeling that three good, stout A&A's would wake Slim up.

They did. He flinched so hard, he jerked the wheel to the right and skewered me with a glare. "Quit barking inside the pickup!"

Yes, but...good grief, we were heading toward the ditch!

Just in time, he jerked the wheel and got us back on the road. "One of these days, you're going to get us killed. Now hush."

Well, that flopped and we were back to Iron Discipline, and we're talking about the very ironist of Iron Discipline, the kind of rigid self-control unknown to your ordinary run of mutts. The technical term for it is Mind Over Easy. Mud Over Matter. Mind Under Water. Skip it.

Wait. *Mind Over Matter*, there we go.

Have you detected that I was feeling nervous about this? I was. I mean, we were creeping along the county road at FIFTEEN MILES AN HOUR and still had another mile to go! I didn't dare bark again, so I beamed him a look of Utter Sincerity that said, "Will you quit poking around and speed this thing up?"

It didn't work, of course. Looks of Utter

Sincerity don't work unless our people are paying attention, and he wasn't. He had fallen back into the bottomless well of his own private thoughts.

I would have to tough it out, endure one more mile of misery. It would be one of the sternest tests of my whole career. To be honest, I wasn't sure I could pull it off. I mean, bad things were going on down there in the dungeon of my body. Just in case the situation blew up, I began rehearsing my story:

"Slim, we've been friends a long time, right? And we're talking about the kind of serious bonding that only happens between a cowboy and his dog. Okay, remember those gizzards you pitched out the back door? You warned me not to eat them, but here's a blast of truth: I disobeyed your orders and, well, ate them anyway.

"It was a careless, bone-head decision and it pretty muchly explains the material you see on your windshield and dashboard. I'm afraid that some of it might have leaked into the defroster vents, and we might have lost the radio too.

"Old friend, dearest pal, cowboy companion, I want you to know HOW SORRY I am about this whole situation. I am desolate, devoured by grief and remorse, hardly able to drag myself through another hour of life."

Would it sell? Maybe. Probably not.

We were still a half-mile away from headquarters, and still poking along at fifteen miles an hour. Okay, I would have to double-down on the Iron Discipline and make sure that we didn't have any disasters.

I filled my tanks with a large gulp of carbon diego and stared straight ahead. I saw...stale bacon grease oozing down the windshield. The world seemed to be drifting out of focus. Suddenly, I felt hot and my head began moving up and down...

Uh oh.

CHAPTER EIGHT

A Roadside Incident

At this point, you're probably in a state of nervous expectoration. Me too. I mean, the stakes were so high on this deal, failure would be Buzzard Bad, the kind of tragedy that can change lives in mere seconds.

We've come this far with the story, but do we dare to go on? Can we tough it out a while longer? I guess we might as well give it a shot and go plunging to the Great Unknown.

Okay, there we were, chugging down the county road at the pace of a turtle. Slim was lost in his thoughts and I was lost in a raging storm that was sweeping me into places I didn't want to go.

The cab was hot, stuffy, suffocating, and the world had taken on the look of oozing bacon grease. Unseen forces deep inside my body had taken control. My head began moving up and down and I began hearing those dreaded sounds.

Ump. Ump. Ump.

Are you sure we ought to go on with this? I mean, when a dog starts making those noises, it's usually too late to put the toothpaste back into the frying pan.

What do you think? Keep going? Okay, you asked for it.

Somewhere in the echoing chambers of my caverns, I heard a man's voice, a loud harsh voice. *"Hank, don't you dare!"*

Was he joking? Whatever it was that I wasn't supposed to "dare" had moved beyond my control. I had become as helpless as a feather in a tornado.

I heard the screech of brakes and felt myself being launched into the dashboard. On another occasion, I might have cared. This time, I didn't care.

I heard a door open and got the impression that someone was dragging me across the floorboard. At that point, everything became a blur. Then...an explosion...several explosions... awful noises...and it was over.

I blinked my eyes and looked around. I was sitting on the side of the road. Drover was looking out the pickup window, staring at me with full-moon eyes. Slim stood nearby. He gazed down at something in the grass. His face collapsed into an expression of...I don't know how to describe it, a look of horror or disbelief, I suppose, and his eyes rolled up inside his head.

"Good honk, you...you ate those gizzards?"

Since the evidence was right there in the grass for the whole world to see, this seemed a good time to be honest. I lifted my head to an angle that expressed...well, grim determination, I suppose.

"Yes, I ate them. It was one of the dumbest stunts I've ever pulled, and that is really saying something, because...it kills me to admit this...I have done this sort of thing before. You might even say that I have a long, gloomy history of Dietary Mistakes."

There, it was out in the open.

You know, if Drover had done something like this, we all would have shrugged and said, "Well, he's just Drover and what do you expect?" But this had happened to ME, the Head of the Entire Security Division!

And don't forget that I had been warned. Oh yes, Slim and Drover had done their best to warn me, but had I listened to my very best friends? Of course not. I had even been warned by a nincompoop buzzard, and that really ripped me.

Fellers, when buzzards come out looking smarter than dogs, this world has sunk about as low as it can sink.

And you know what else? I couldn't even blame this one on the cat! The little sneak had been two miles away, at ranch headquarters.

So there's the Awful Reality I faced in a ditch on the side of the county road, in the middle of a spirit-killing drought, and expressed it with Saddest Eyes and Wags of Repentance on the tail section. The presentation left me feeling empty, exhausted, used up, defeated, and as worthless as spilled milk.

Slim had buried his face in his hands and was shaking his head. How do you suppose that made me feel? Terrible.

Well, it was clear what had to be done. I had made a complete dunce of myself and disgraced my ranch. I would have to resign my commission with the Security Division, empty my desk, and move on to a new life as...I didn't know what, as a hermit-dog, a wanderer, a lost soul in the night.

Some dogs have no sense of shame, you know, and they'll try to hang onto their job after a scandal. Me? I'd always served my ranch with pride, and the other side of cowdog pride is

SHAME. When you mess up big-time and make a dunce of yourself, you should feel ashamed. No arguments, no phony excuses. Admit your mistakes and move out. It's the only decent thing to do.

I rose to my feet, caught Drover's eye and told him farewell in a glance, turned toward the north, and began my long and lonely journey into exile. I had gone, oh, ten steps, when I heard a voice behind me.

"Hey! Where do you think you're going?"

I turned and looked back at Slim, that dear friend from my Days Before Disgrace. He had taken his hands away from his face. He had a kind face unless you saw it in the middle of the night, and then he looked quite a bit like a vampire.

Where I was going? Away. Into the wilderness. Into exile.

"Come here."

No, there was nothing left to say.

He patted his thigh. "Come here."

Okay, but I couldn't stay long.

With my head hanging so low that my nose was bumping weeds, I trudged back to my former friend, knowing full well that this was futile. Two feet away from him, I stopped and went into the Crushed Spirit Wagging Sequence on the tail section.

He knelt down (his knees popped, as usual) and patted his thigh again. "Come here."

Well...okay. I moved closer and was shocked and a little worried when he reached out, grabbed one of my legs, and pulled me into his arms. I mean, he wrapped me up in both arms and pulled me into a...this sounds crazy, but he seemed to have pulled me into a HUG. He even pressed his cheek against the top of my head.

What was going on here?

"Pooch, it wasn't entirely your fault. What kind of knucklehead keeps rotten food in his ice box? Me." He rubbed me behind the ears. "You ain't a perfect dog, Hankie, and I'm at least two-days' ride from being a perfect man, but we can't just curl up and die. Maybe we ought to move on and try to do better, you reckon?"

Well...maybe...okay. Yes!

He offered his hand. "Shake on it. You remember how to shake hands?"

Of course I remembered how to shake hands, but this occasion called for more than a handshake. I flew into the middle of him and began licking his face and ears.

"For Pete's sake, don't lick me with that tongue!"

Hey, it was the only tongue I had, and we were friends again and I still had my job! Oh, happy day!

Old Slim laughed, grabbed me around the middle, and for several minutes, we rolled around in the ditch, laughing and growling and celebrating our New Beginning. We were so carried away that neither one of us heard the pickup or noticed the man who was standing over us.

Loper. The boss. He cleared his throat. "Did I come at a bad time?"

Slim stopped wrestling, rose to his feet, brushed the grass off his jeans, and picked up his hat. "Yes, but I know you love catching me in awkward moments."

A grin tugged at Lipper's lopes...at Loper's lips, that is. "I do, and we have so many of them out here. Sometimes I wonder if this is a working cattle ranch or school for unemployed clowns."

"I've wondered about that myself."

"Should I ask what's going on here?"

"No, let's skip it."

Loper squinted toward the, uh, material in the ditch. "What's that?"

"Leftovers from breakfast. You want a bite?"

Loper made a sour face. "The dog?"

"Yes. He got into some gizzards that were a little past their prime."

Loper shook his head. "Bachelors. It's a wonder you're still alive."

74

Slim hitched up his jeans. "Reckon we could change the subject? How come you're out so early? Did Sally May run you out of the house?"

"Did you happen to catch the local news this morning?"

"I try to avoid the news."

"Well, there's a mountain lion in the area, and it ran a hundred head of steers through a fence last night."

"Where?"

"Dave Nicholson's place."

Slim's eyebrows rose. "That's pretty close."

"And I found some big tracks up by the machine shed."

"In mud or dust?"

"Mud."

"So they're fresh, made after that little shower."

Loper nodded. "That's right. Now, I don't want to interrupt your playtime with the dogs, but if you can work it into your schedule, maybe you could saddle a horse and get a count on our yearlings."

"Loper, you've got such a sweet way of putting things."

"I learned it from my banker. He still thinks we're running a cattle operation out here. See you at headquarters, and hurry up, first chance you get."

Loper headed for his pickup, and Slim and I loaded up in his. When Drover saw me coming, he sprinted over to the passenger-side window. "I get dibs on Shotgun! Hee hee."

"You'll get dibs on a fat lip if you don't mind your manners." I shoved him over to the middle, where he belonged. "Did you hear what Loper said?"

"Yeah, you barfed up your toenails. I knew you would."

"That's not what he said."

"But at least you didn't do it in the pickup."

"Hello? Is anyone home in there?"

He glanced around. "Where?"

"Inside that skull of yours."

"Oh yeah, I stay there sometimes."

"Good. Listen up. We've just gotten a report that we might have a mountain lion on the ranch."

His eyes shorted out. "A mountain lion! Oh my gosh, what'll we do?"

That was the question that faced the Security Division. And I didn't have a good answer.

CHAPTER NINE

Something Lurking
in the Machine Shed

When we arrived at the machine shed, Loper was standing beside his pickup, tapping his toe, glancing at his watch, and checking the angle of the sun. We got out and joined him.

"They say it takes eight minutes for sunlight to reach the earth."

Slim gave him a blank look. "Good."

"That's 93 million miles. It took *you* eight minutes to drive half a mile to headquarters."

"Well, I ain't a sunbeam."

Loper grunted. "Truer words were never spoken. You know, that pickup can go faster than ten miles an hour. If it's not running right, we can take it to a mechanic."

"I had it up to seventeen going down a hill.

What's the rush?"

"That mountain lion is the rush. It has probably run half our yearlings through the fence. Let's look at those tracks."

We followed him around to the east side of the machine shed. In a good year, that area would have been grown up in weeds, but now, in the drought, it was just another patch of dirt on a ranch that had a lot of them.

Loper stopped and pointed at tracks in the mud. Slim leaned over and studied them. "Those are dog tracks."

"What makes you think so?"

"Because they are."

"Our dogs don't have feet that big."

"Well, that gives you a clue. You've got a big dog running a-loose on the ranch. Big dogs make big dog tracks."

Loper gave him a sour look. "You're just a regular Sherlock Holmes, aren't you?"

"Loper, when a man slows down and opens his eyes, he sees things. It's kind of amazing. You ought to try it sometime."

Loper grumbled under his breath and looked away. "If this world depended on you, clocks would run backwards and we'd still be living in holes."

Slim gave me a wink and a grin. "He has a

terrible time admitting that he's wrong. Let's try to be patient. Shhh."

"All right, maybe they're dog tracks. Find the dog and we'll try to locate the owner."

"Thanks, boss, I know that hurt."

"It did, but I'll feel better when I take it out of your paycheck. Ha!" Loper headed toward the house.

Slim looked down at me. "He wouldn't dock my paycheck, would he?"

How was I supposed to know? The way those two carried on, a dog never knew what to believe.

Slim tugged on his chin. "Well, how do we find one dog on a ten-section ranch?"

Easy. Food.

"I can't spend the whole day ahorseback, looking for dog tracks."

Food. Put out some food.

He snapped his fingers. "Wait a second, I've got it. I'll put out some food." He tapped himself on the head. "Old Slim has more tricks than Harry Hoodunnit. Heh."

Oh brother. Of course he gave me no credit for coming up with the idea. Oh well.

He ducked into the machine shed and came out with half a sack of Co-op dog food. He held it a couple of feet above the Ford hubcap that served as our food bowl, and poured out a stream of kernels that made a loud pinging sound.

My tongue shot out, mopping my lips, and I headed straight for...

"Hank! This ain't for you."

Huh? Well, sure, I knew that. I just thought... gee, what a grouch.

Anyway, Slim had baited the trap, so to speak, and now all we had to do was wait for the mutt to show up. "Pooch, you stand guard and I'll do chores. If he shows up, give me a bark."

Aye aye, sir!

"And don't eat the dog food."

Bummer.

Slim went down to the corrals to feed the horses, and I went on Guard Duty, pacing back and forth in front of the machine shed. Minutes passed, and it began to look like a ho-hum operation. The longer I waited, the more nobody showed up, and that gave us a major clue in the case: if we had a stray mutt on the ranch, it wasn't Happy Lab.

Remember him? He showed up one day, wearing a bird cage on his head. A typical Labrador, he ate all the time, non-stop, and he could smell food if you put it on the moon. If Hap had been the stray dog, he would have showed up two seconds after the first kernel hit the food bowl.

Hencely, we could cross Happy Lab off the list of suspects.

You're probably wondering what Drover was doing during all of this. When we arrived at headquarters, he scampered straight into the machine shed and hid. Why? Because he'd heard two words that scared him wrong-side out: mountain lion. He's such a little chicken.

But then I heard his voice. "Hank? Pssst. We need to talk."

My eyelids sprang open (perhaps I had dozed) and I glanced around. Okay, there was Drover standing in the crack between the big sliding doors. I went through the Stretch and Yawn Procedure, and marched over to him. "Okay, talk."

It was then I noticed that he looked scared, and we're talking about trembling and moon-eyed. "Hank, you know that mountain lion? Well, I f-f-found him. He's in the machine shed!"

Several thousand volts of electrical current sizzled down my backbone. "Good grief, are you sure about that?"

His teeth were clacking together. "No question. Huge, tan color, long tail, horrible green eyes!"

"Holy smokes, that's a mountain lion all right. Did he growl at you?"

"Oh yeah! Well..."

"Well what?"

"He didn't exactly growl."

"What exactly did he do?"

"Well, he...he told me to go away and leave him alone."

"Drover, that's not even close to a growl."

"Well, it scared me half to death."

I heaved a sigh. "Son, we've got a stray dog hiding in the machine shed."

"Gosh, what'll we do?"

I laid a paw on his shoulder. "I'm glad you asked, because we need a brave soldier to lead a scout patrol."

He stared at me with crossed eyes, then collapsed like a chunk of cement. "Oh rats, this old leg just went out on me! Oh, the pain!"

"Just what I figured. Never mind."

I stepped over my quivering assistant and entered the machine shed. Behind me, I heard him say, "The guilt is eating me up!"

Worthless.

I made my way past the cutting torch, the welder, and all the tools and junk the cowboys had left after their last repair job, and headed toward the dark, remote part of the shed, back where Sally May kept her grandmother's furniture and Loper kept his canvas-covered canoe.

All the while, my eyes were probing the gloom until...*there he was*! A large creature, tan in color, lying in the shadowy shadows, staring at me with cruel green eyes, and...

Hang on to something. I don't want to scare you, but all of a sudden it hit me like a cinder block. I was looking straight into the eyes of A MOUNTAIN LION!

I stopped and tried to swallow the dry lump that had formed in the throatalary region of my throat. My mind was tumbling. I mean, this was very confusing. First we'd thought it was a mountain lion, then a stray dog, and now we were back to a mountain lion.

And fellers, if I was alone in a dark machine shed with a mountain lion, we had a serious problem.

Should we go on with this or shut everything down? You know how I am about the children. I don't mind giving them a little buzz every now and then, but when it comes to the dark and scary parts of my work...

Look, we could do something else and nobody needs to know. We could hide under the bed, eat cookies, play Tug the Sock, anything to take our minds off of what might have been lurking in the gloomy depths of the machine shed.

What do you think?

Keep going?

Okay, you were warned. Take a deep seat. I hope we make it through this thing in one piece. Or even two or three pieces. I mean, mountain lions aren't play-like bad guys. They're the real thing.

CHAPTER TEN

You'll Never Guess What It Was

A re you ready? Okay, let's set the scenery again.

There I was in the gloomy depths of the machine shed, and I had just picked up SOMETHING on Visual Radar. The VizRad image showed something big and alive, but was it a mountain lion?

It was time to run a test. I hide to try the quiver in my...tried to hide the quiver voice and switched on the microphone. "Hello there, whoever you are. I'm with the ranch's Security Division and we heard you were in here. Sure enough, you are and, well, we'd like to check some identification. Just routine."

I heard nothing but my own heart banging in

the silence.

"Look, if this is a bad time, we don't have to make it a big deal. Just say something to let us know who you are and we'll be done with it."

No answer, and I could feel a strip of hair rising along my backbone. Something was very wrong about this. Had I been lured into a trap by a huge, cunning predator cat, the same kind of beast that could stalk, chase down, and kill a full-grown deer?

These thoughts were racing down the dark alley of my mind when I heard a sound...maybe a ferocious growl. And fellers, things came apart. My eyes popped out of their sprockets and my ears almost flew off my head and the Emergency Sprinkler System went off.

I hit Turbo Six and headed for the door, tripped on the rubble Slim and Loper had left in the middle of the floor, got cart-wheeled, went down, jumped up, and scrambled toward daylight. Just before I was about to explode through the crack between the doors, a thought popped up inside my head:

"Mountain lions scream. What you heard was a croaky growl. It's a dog, Meathead."

Huh?

I hit Air Brakes Lockdown and skidded to a

stop. A cloud of white smoke rose from all four paws. My whole body was shaking. I turned around and faced the Abyss.

"One last question. Are you a mountain lion?"

An answer came from the gloom. "Maybe. Go away and leave me alone."

Air hissed out of my lungs and I slumped to the floor. I lay there for a full minute, panting and staring at nothing, then climbed back to my feet.

"By any chance, is your name Happy Lab?"

"How'd you know?"

"What in thunder are you doing here?"

"Nothing. Go away."

I marched toward the sound of his voice and located him near the northwest corner, the same gloomy region where Drover often went to escape Life Itself. As I approached, Happy Lab gave me a mournful look and began whapping his tree-limb tail on the floor.

Bam. Bam. Bam.

I towered over him and tried to get a handle on my temper. "Listen, buster, you just blew all the circuits on our Early Warning Systems, and you WILL explain yourself."

"I'd rather not."

"Too bad. Nobody on this ranch cares what you want. Talk."

His gaze wandered. "We were having a picnic at the lake."

"And let me guess. You wandered off and got lost? Again?"

He shook his head. "Not lost. I just left."

I began pacing, as I often do when I'm suspecting an interrogator...interrogating a suspect, shall we say. "The lake is two miles away. Did you walk?"

"I saw a pickup and hopped into the back. I wanted to hide."

"And then?"

"Some guy got in and drove off."

"You didn't know him?"

"No sir. Never expected that he'd drive off. It kind of threw me for a loop."

"Yeah, well, you've got lots of loops, Happy, and I've seen a few of them. Go on with your story."

"Well, he drove a ways, then had to slow down to let some horses cross the road."

"Okay, I'm seeing a pattern here. You were in our horse pasture and the horses were coming in to water. Go on."

"I jumped out and he drove off, and there I was on the side of the road. I saw this barn and it looked familiar, so I came and hid. I didn't want anyone to find me, but you did."

I stopped pacing and glared down at him. "Of course I found you! This is my ranch and I know everything that goes on. I knew you were here before you knew it yourself. The only thing I don't know is why you're hiding in my machine shed."

"I can't explain it."

"Try. And hurry up. I've got a ranch to run."

"I hate being a burden."

"Talk!"

"Okay." His eyes drifted around. "All my life, I've wanted to make my people happy, especially the kids. And I've got what you might call a gift. Any time they're hurt or sad, I can put my head in their lap, look into their eyes, wag my tail, and somehow it makes everything okay."

By this time, my eyes had adjusted to the half-darkness and I found myself looking into his face. You know what? He had the sweetest, kindest face I had ever seen on a dog, honest, serene, loyal, and caring. It must have been part of what he called his "gift." Most dogs don't have it...and wish they did.

"So what happened? What are you doing here?"

His head sank. "My gift quit me. Little Rachel needed me and I failed."

"Who is Little Rachel?"

"One of the girls in the family. She's six." His

eyes filled with mist. "She fell out of a tree and broke her arm."

"This morning? At the picnic?"

He nodded. "Her arm was all bent and crooked, and she cried something awful. It tore my heart to see her in such pain...but I couldn't make it go away. I couldn't make it all right!"

"So...they took her to the doctor and you jumped into the back of a stranger's pickup and ran away from home, and here you are? That's it?"

"Yes sir. I couldn't fix it. I failed. I'm just a worthless mutt."

"Well, here's a news flash. You're not a doctor, Hap. You're just a dog."

"Yeah, well, they need to find a better dog."

Did I have time to talk sense to this big galoot? No, but I did it anyway. I began pacing a circle around him, as I often do when I feel a lecture coming on.

"Hap, let me tell you something. The first time you showed up out here, I was so jealous, I could hardly see straight."

"Aw heck. Jealous of me?"

"That's correct. See, you Labs can do ridiculous things twenty-four hours a day, and people don't care. They'll forgive you for anything."

"You think so?"

"I know so. I've seen it with my own eyes. You guys have some kind of slippery charm that never seems to fail. You've got it made, pal. The rest of us have to work for a living. I wish I could buy a bottle of your charm and use it on Sally May."

"You...you think my family might want me back?"

"Duh! Of course they'll want you back! When they leave the doctor's office, they'll be driving the roads, looking for you. Children will be weeping in the back seat and the ladies will be wringing their hands."

"Over me?"

"Roger that, and sooner or later, they'll show up out here. Not only will they take you back, they'll love you more than ever." I stopped pacing and whirled around. "But they'll never find you if you're hiding in the machine shed, feeling sorry for yourself."

"Is that what I'm doing?"

"Absolutely, yes. Here you are, moping because you can't wag your tail three times and fix a child's broken arm."

"It sounds silly when you put it that way."

I stuck my nose in his face. "Hap, you're not a magician. You do a great job of being the family dog, and that's all you get. Shape up."

"Well, maybe you're right. Okay. I'm sorry."
He rose to his feet and glanced around. "Say,
what time do y'all eat breakfast around here?"

I had to laugh. I knew he was feeling better.
"Come on, Big Boy, I'll show you the grub. You
can't fix a broken arm, but I know you can fix a
bowl of dog food."

"I love to eat, I won't deny that."

We left the gloom of the machine shed and
stepped outside into the sunlight. I grabbed a big
gulp of dry desert air. Well! I had pulled Happy
Lab through a little crisis and had proved, once
and forever, that we didn't have a mountain lion
on the ranch

Everything had returned to normal, and that
sounds like a good place to end the story.

Why don't we just close the curtains and turn
off the lights?

This case is...

Wait, not so fast. There's more, and I must
warn you. It will get scarier than you think.

CHAPTER ELEVEN

Kitty Makes a Confession

The moment Happy Lab stepped outside, his bird dog nose picked up the scent of food. His eyes went straight to the dog bowl and he mopped a string of drool off his lips. "You go first. It's your ranch."

"No, you go first. I've had a little indigestion this morning."

"Huh. Sorry to hear that. Something you ate?"

"Yes. Something I ate tried to eat me back."

"Aw heck. Yeah, that happens sometimes." He kept staring at the hubcap and mopped his chops again. "Sure you don't want to go first?"

"No, go ahead. Just leave a little snack at the bottom for me."

"Got it."

He lumbered over to the overturned Ford hubcap and went to work on the Co-op. While he wolfed and crunched, I caught a glimpse of a nose and a pair of eyes peeking around the southeast corner of the barn. Then I heard Mister Shivers say, "Is it safe to come out?"

"Yes, all clear." Drover came padding over to me and I pointed to the Lab. "That's your so-called mountain lion."

Drover stared. "Oh, I'm so glad! You wouldn't believe how scared I was."

"Of course I would believe it. Being scared is what you do for a living."

"You weren't scared? Tell the truth."

"Not even for a second. In fact, I was kind of looking forward to duking it out with a cougar. They're not as tough as they think."

"Yeah, neither am I, and I don't even think I'm tough." He glanced down toward the house. "Oh look, Little Alfred's coming out to play. Here I go!"

He went hopping down to the yard, just in time to greet our little pal as he pushed open the gate. Well, that was something Drover could do, greet the children in the morning.

Happy Lab had joined me by then, licking the crumbs off his mouth. "Hank, we need to talk. I...I forgot to leave you a snack. Sorry. Sometimes

I get carried away over breakfast."

"Yes, I've noticed. Oh well, at least you didn't eat the hubcap."

"Say what?"

"At least you didn't eat the bowl."

"Oh no, I never eat the bowl." His gaze swept the horizon. "Say, what time do y'all eat lunch?"

"That was it, Hap, breakfast, lunch, and maybe supper too. And by the way, don't even think about diving over the garden fence and eating Sally May's tomatoes and squash."

He flinched. "How'd you know?"

I laughed. "Hap, you have an honest face. You can't hide anything."

"Yes sir. I'll stay out of the garden. I'll try to stay out of the garden." His eyes lingered on the garden. "I'll sure try."

I stepped into the path of his gaze. "Stay. Out. Of. The. Garden."

"Yes sir, got it."

"Let's go find Slim. He'll want to know you're here...again."

"I hope I'm not a burden."

What a guy. I must admit, it was kind of fun to have him back on the ranch.

We trotted down the hill and found Slim in the corral, breaking a bale of prairie hay and tossing it into the hay feeder.

When he saw Happy, he nodded and smiled. "Him again? Heh. Didn't I call it? Mountain lion. Loper needs to go to tracking school." He rubbed me on the ears. "Nice work, Hankie, I owe you a gizzard or two."

Gag. Did we need to talk about that? I was still recovering from the last round of his gizzards.

Slim hitched up his jeans. (They always seemed to be slipping down). "Well, David and Sandra will be looking for Bird Cage. I'll tell Loper to give 'em a call, so they won't be worrying."

Through Wags and Ears, I tried to give him the message that the Sells' daughter had broken her arm and they might be at the hospital for a while. It was a difficult message, pretty complicated, and I waited to see if he understood it.

No. It went right past him. Oh well.

At that very moment, Happy cut loose with a deep bark. ROOF! I turned and saw that he had stiffened into the Alert Position. His head was up, his ears were up, his nose was working, and his tail had become a straight stick, pointing due south. Then, suddenly, he dashed off to the north.

Slim had been watching too. "Huh. Something sure woke him up. We'd better go check, pooch.

I'd hate for him to get skunked or porcupined."

Good point. Some dogs don't have enough sense to stay away from a creature that waddles around and doesn't fight. As a matter of fact... never mind. The point is that you'll never go broke underestimating the intelligence of a bird dog. I mean, this was the same dog that ate raw tomatoes, squash, and okra.

We headed north, up a ravine and through a grove of chinaberry trees, following the roar of Happy's barks. We found him standing over a pile of leaves and grass, barking his head off and swinging his tail. Slim looked at the ground, then up into the trees. No skunk or porcupine.

"Well, it must have been a bird. Come on, dogs, we've got work to do."

Hap didn't want to leave, but he did, and we followed Slim back to the house. I asked, "What was that all about?"

"I caught the scent of a deer and follered it right to that spot."

"In this drought, they come into headquarters for water."

"He sure left a strong scent."

"I'm glad you enjoyed it."

When we reached the yard, Slim went inside the house to tell Loper that we had found his

"mountain lion," and that David and Sandra Sell's yellow Lab had wandered back into our lives.

Hap and I sat down at the yard gate, and I noticed that he seemed...I don't know, distracted or deep in thought, not a normal condition for your bird dog breeds.

"What's wrong with you?"

"Huh? Me? Oh nothing." He was silent for a moment. "Well...there was something kind of funny back there. It had a powerful-strong smell of deer...but there was more. I smelled a cat too."

"A cat?"

"Yes sir, and the signal was strong."

"Well, we can clear that up in a hurry. I just happen to have a suspect."

I marched down the fence until I was standing directly west of the iris patch. I couldn't see him, but I knew he was in there. "Pete? I know you never get out of bed before noon, but we need to have a word."

Sure enough, his cunning little eyes appeared through the stalks of the iris plants, and I heard his whiney voice. "Well, well! It's Hankie the Wonderdog...with a friend."

"Front and center, Kitty, and hurry up."

"Does that mean 'please'?"

"It means I'm a very busy dog."

He came sliding out of the iris patch, and there was no "hurry up" in the way he moved. My lips quivered, aching to show fangs, but I managed to keep them under control.

See, I knew what he was up to. He does it all the time. The little pestilence knows that it drives me NUTS to wait for a cat, so he turns it into a production of Kitty Theater and drags it out as long as he can.

It took him half an hour to slither from the iris patch over to the fence. Okay, maybe it was only thirty seconds, but when you're waiting for a cat, every second is a minute and every minute is an hour. I hate it.

Finally he rubbed up against the fence and beamed me his usual insolent smirk. "Here...I... am."

"Well, did you enjoy your disgusting little parade through the yard?"

"I did, Hankie, and I'm so glad you noticed. Somehow it just..." He fluttered his eyelashes. "...well, it brings a burst of meaning into my little life. What can I do for you this morning?"

"I'll ask the questions, Kitty. Our Special Crimes Unit has been doing some undercover work."

"How exciting!"

"We have reason to believe that sometime in the past twelve hours, you were stalking a deer about thirty yards north of the corrals."

"Really!"

"Question One: is it true?"

"No."

I turned to Hap. "Bingo. It was him." Back to the cat. "Let's move on to Question Two: Why would a little dink of a cat try to stalk a deer?"

"Well, Hankie..."

"If you caught one, what would you do with it? Stick with birds, Pete, or maybe grasshoppers."

"But Hankie..."

"Don't harass the deer. Sally May likes to watch them when they come up around headquarters."

His weird kitty eyes swept from me to Hap and back to me. "Hankie, I'm just amazed that you figured it out."

"Ha! So you're finally going to admit it?"

"I might as well come clean." He rolled his eyes up to the sky. "Yes, I was stalking a deer. Doesn't every twelve-pound cat dream of capturing a hundred-pound deer?"

I turned to Hap. "See? He has delusions." I whirled back to the cat. "That will be all, Kitty, you're excused. Go back to your spider web."

I marched away, leaving Sally May's rotten

little cat sitting in the shamble of his own ramble. My interrogation had turned him wrong-side-out.

Wow. Was that awesome or what? Sometimes I even scare myself.

CHAPTER TWELVE

An Amazing Twist in the Case, Wow!

Happy and I made our way back to the yard gate. "There you go, Hap, that's how it's done in Big Time law enforcement."

"He was lying. It wasn't him."

I stopped. "What?"

"The cat I smelled wasn't him."

I hosed him with a scowl. "Hap, I don't mind you tagging along on my rounds, but leave the heavy lifting to me, okay? Pete made a confession. I hammered it out of him. Why would he confess if he didn't do it?"

He shrugged. "I don't know. Because he's a cat?"

All at once I found myself wondering...hmmm. In the courthouse basement of my mind, I went back to the transcript of my interrogation of Kitty Precious and began looking for bupp, excuse me, looking for holes in his cheese... holes in his confession.

Happy's nose took an upward jerk. "Hey, I smell cheese."

"You smell what's left of moldy chicken gizzards."

"No kidding?" His eyes lit up. "You got any left?"

"Listen, pal, if you think that smells good, I don't need to trust anything you say about the scent of a cat. Let's drop it. Leave the cats to me."

"Yes sir. Sorry. I don't want to get in the way."

At that moment, Drover and Alfred came around the south side of the house. When Alfred saw Happy Lab, he squealed with joy, ran to him, and engulfed him in a hug. Hap swang his tree-limb tail back and...

Wait. Hold it, halt. Swang? We need to check the grammar on that.

Ring, rang, rung
Swim, swam, swum
Bing, bang, bum
Swing, swang, swung

Okay, that checks out. Happy swang his tail back and forth and licked the boy's face from chin to ear, then Alfred climbed on his back and they played Horsie.

Drover drifted over to me and we watched. Drover said, "He sure is good with kids, isn't he?"

"He's the best, and it eats my liver."

"Gosh, how come?"

"Drover, look at him. He's always so good, kind, gentle, and patient, and he does it without effort. He makes the rest of us look like bums."

"I always wanted to be a bum, but Mom wouldn't stand for it."

"What?"

"I said, when Mom got tired of standing, she'd sit on her bum."

"Of course she did. Where else would she sit?"

"Well, sometimes she sat on the porch. And one time she sat on a scorpion."

"And that proves...what? Is there a point to this conversation?"

"Don't sit on a scorpion...I guess."

I gazed into the depths of his eyes and suddenly realized...*there was nothing in there!* I had no idea how we had gotten on the subject of scorpions, but somehow...oh well.

Where were we? Oh yes, Happy Lab was

giving Alfred a horsie ride, and the mutt was such a great sport, it almost made me ill. I know that sounds like petty jealousy, but the truth is... okay, it was petty jealousy, might as well come clean. I'm not a perfect dog. Neither was Happy Lab, but he came a lot closer than I did.

At last Hap got tired and sat down, and Alfred got dumped on the ground. Hap smiled, thumped his tail, and panted for air with five inches of tongue hanging out the left side of his mouth.

Alfred dusted himself off and turned to me. "I got bucked off."

Right. Bucked off, but good ride.

"Y'all dogs want to go for a hike?"

A hike? Sure. Hiking was something I could do better than any Lab ever built.

And so it was that the four of us set out on an Exploration of Ranch Headquarters. Alfred took the lead position and I stationed myself right beside him. Drover came second, where he belonged, and Hap brought up the rear.

Hiking wasn't Happy's best event, don't you see, because he was a big dog...and don't forget, he was packing about fifty pounds of Co-op dog food.

We made our way Out West, past Emerald Pond and through that grove of big Chinese elm trees, past the saddle shed, through the corrals, onward to the north. We were making our way through a grove of chinaberry trees when Happy kicked up his pace to a lope and chugged past us.

Up ahead, he stopped at that same pile of leaves and grass where he'd found the scent of a deer. Remember that? I had almost forgotten about it, but when we got there, he was digging into the mound, and we're talking about serious digging with leaves and twigs flying.

Then he stopped and poked his nose into the mound. "I knew it! There's a deer under all this stuff."

I rushed forward and pushed him out of the way. "I'll take it from here, Hap." Actually, I *tried* to push him out of the way. If you've ever tried to move a Lab, you know that they're about as movable as a cement pillar.

Even so, I did a quick study of the scene and came to an astounding conclusion. "There's a deer buried under this pile of leaves!"

Hap nodded. "That's what I said, and it's dead too."

"Hap, I'm on it, okay? Regardless of what you say, this deer is *dead*."

He lifted his nose and began sniffing. "Yeah, and remember that cat smell I picked up before? Well, I'm picking it up again…and it's really strong."

I scorched him with a glare. "So what are you saying? That Pete killed a deer and buried it under grass and leaves? That is totally ridiculous. Pete's too much of a slacker to kill a mouse, much less a deer."

"I didn't say it was Pete."

"Oh? Then maybe you'd like to tell this court who or whom might have killed the deer—since we have no other cats on this ranch!"

His eyes were sweeping the area. "Do you know what kind of cat kills a deer and buries it under grass and leaves? A mountain lion."

A surge of electrical currency crackled down my backbone. I shot a glance at Drover and noticed...gee, not much, just several dog hairs floating in the spot where he had been only seconds before. I mean, he had evaporated, poof, and was highballing it back to the machine shed.

My mouth had gone dry. "Wait a second. Are you saying..."

"We need to get out of here. Now."

"Hap, I'm giving the orders. On my mark, we will do an about-face and make an orderly..."

My words were obittilated...obiturated... phooey...my words were drowned by a SCREAM that made every hair on my back stand straight up, an unearthly scream full of horror and menace.

Then...hang on...then a huge shadowy form crept toward us out of the trees. It had green eyes. It was a mountain lion, the real thing.

Alfred saw it too, and I heard the air rushing into his chest. "Hankie! It's a tiger!"

My mind was in a swirl. "Hap, do these guys eat kids?"

"Don't know, man, but we can't chance it. You take the boy and run. I'll lay down some cover fire."

"Are you sure?"

He shrugged. "I'm the big guy. Y'all scram."

"Good plan." I turned to the boy and gave him an expression that said, "Run! Run for your life!"

We turned south and went plunging through the trees, and made it back to the corrals. There, I stopped and looked north. The monster hadn't followed us, and I could hear Hap laying down his biggest barks. Did I dare go back and help?

Uh...no. Hap would be fine.

But wait! Just then I heard footsteps coming from the south. I turned and saw...holy smokes, it was Slim and Loper! They'd heard the screams of the cat and were coming in a dead run, and by George, they had armed themselves with clubs.

I took a big gulp of air and courage came rushing back. Happy Lab needed help. I turned to the north and hit Full Turbos. When I got there, Hap and the cat were facing each other, Hap pumping out his biggest barks and the cat swatting at him with a huge paw.

The cat didn't notice me, and I went straight to the part of his body that seemed most vulnerable: his long tail. I cranked open my enormous jaws and slammed them shut. Wow. That got his attention. He growled and whirled, slung me around like a paper doll, and tried to tear my head off with his claws, only he couldn't reach me.

"Take that, you big bully!"

Hee hee. I love mouthing off to a...

BAM!

He knocked a slat out of me, and when I staggered to my feet, old Hap was right there beside me—grinning like a lunatic. "He's made me mad now. Let's beat the snot out of him."

"I've got a better idea. Let's get out of here!"

"Naw, I want a piece of this guy." He squared his shoulders and faced the dragon, and believe it or not, his face still held the sweetness that is so natural to Labs. "Come on, Kitty, pick on someone your own size." And he stepped toward the beast.

I was shocked. The mutt either had big courage or big stupid.

I'm sorry to report that Hap got decked on the first punch, and we're talking about smeared. It was a solid left hook, and it didn't matter that Hap thought he was a big guy and pretty tough. He went rolling like a big rubber ball, and the cougar was poised to finish him off.

Well, back to work. That Reverse Strangle Hold had worked pretty well in Round One (go for the tail instead of the throat, don't you see), so I went back to it, took a big bite on his tail, and hung on. The monster swung me in circles and it gave Hap enough time to catch his wind, and he came back into the brawl.

You know, if the cowboys had given us just one more minute, we would have...okay, might as well be honest about this. In another minute, we would have been *cat food*, period. I mean, that cougar was a man among boys. In a fair fight, he would have eaten us for a snack.

But, thank goodness, it wasn't a fair fight. The cowboys arrived and waded in with Clubs That Don't Break, a couple of old bodark posts that were as hard as iron. They started thrashing the cat and landed a couple good ones to his face, and he decided that he could have more fun somewhere else. Like a big tan shadow, he vanished.

Loper and Slim were gasping for air. Between

gasps, Loper said, "Dog tracks, huh?"

"Loper, they were dog tracks. Look it up in your Boy Scout manual."

"So how do you go from dog tracks to a live cougar?"

"Well, I don't know, but it ain't my fault."

"You ought to listen to the news once in a while. It was on the radio."

"I ain't going to listen to the news."

This could have gone on all day, but at that point, they happened to notice the wounded troops lying on the beach, me and Hap. I had been pretty well thumped around, and Hap was bleeding from a gash on his side.

Loper dropped his club and went to him. "Hey, buddy, how you doing?"

In spite of his wounds, Hap gave him a sweet smile and tapped his tail. He tried to stand up, but sank back down.

Loper looked at Slim. "I guess you'll have to carry him."

"Me? What about both of us? He weighs more than I do."

"You are such a panty-waist." Loper pushed Slim out of the way and tried to lift Big Boy, and soon figured out that Hap was a two-man dog. "Reckon you could help?"

"Sure. Panty-waist."

And so it was that we started back to the house—Loper and Slim carrying the Lab and arguing all the way, and me limping along behind. (Notice that nobody volunteered to carry me).

Actually, I had a bunch of bruises, nothing too serious, but Hap had that bad slice on his left side. When we made it back to the house, Loper told Slim to drive Hap to the vet to get some stitches. As they were driving away, Hap was riding in the back of the pickup. He managed to stand up and yell, "I'll be back in time for supper!"

What a guy. Nobody can stay mad at a Lab.

You're probably wondering about Drover. Well, don't waste your sympathy. He stayed holed up in the machine shed for two days, and when he finally crept outside, he might have had bed sores but not a scratch from combat. Sometimes I wonder...oh well.

And that's about the end the story. Happy Lab got patched up and made it back to the ranch in time to scarf down another twenty pounds of Co-op dog food. The next day, David and Sandra Sell drove out to the ranch and picked him up, and their kids squealed with joy and hugged his neck, even little Rachel who was wearing a cast on her arm.

It was kind of amazing, how much they loved that big lug of a Lab.

Well, we had made it through another dangerous day on the ranch. Little Alfred was safe, Sally May was proud, and while she wasn't watching, I settled my accounts with her rotten little cat, tee hee.

Hey, I couldn't whip a mountain lion, but I sure knew how to chase the local cat up a tree. Is that awesome or what?

Thanks for sticking with me through the scary parts. This case is closed.

Have you read all
of Hank's adventures?

1 *The Original Adventures of Hank the Cowdog*
2 *The Further Adventures of Hank the Cowdog*
3 *It's a Dog's Life*
4 *Murder in the Middle Pasture*
5 *Faded Love*
6 *Let Sleeping Dogs Lie*
7 *The Curse of the Incredible Priceless Corncob*
8 *The Case of the One-Eyed Killer Stud Horse*
9 *The Case of the Halloween Ghost*
10 *Every Dog Has His Day*
11 *Lost in the Dark Unchanted Forest*
12 *The Case of the Fiddle-Playing Fox*
13 *The Wounded Buzzard on Christmas Eve*
14 *Hank the Cowdog and Monkey Business* ✓
15 *The Case of the Missing Cat*
16 *Lost in the Blinded Blizzard*
17 *The Case of the Car-Barkaholic Dog*
18 *The Case of the Hooking Bull*
19 *The Case of the Midnight Rustler* ✓
20 *The Phantom in the Mirror*

21 *The Case of the Vampire Cat*

22 *The Case of the Double Bumblebee Sting*

23 *Moonlight Madness*

24 *The Case of the Black-Hooded Hangmans*

25 *The Case of the Swirling Killer Tornado*

26 *The Case of the Kidnapped Collie*

27 *The Case of the Night-Stalking Bone Monster*

28 *The Mopwater Files*

29 *The Case of the Vampire Vacuum Sweeper*

30 *The Case of the Haystack Kitties*

31 *The Case of the Vanishing Fishhook*

32 *The Garbage Monster from Outer Space*

33 *The Case of the Measled Cowboy*

34 *Slim's Good-bye*

35 *The Case of the Saddle House Robbery*

36 *The Case of the Raging Rottweiler*

37 *The Case of the Deadly Ha-Ha Game*

38 *The Fling*

39 *The Secret Laundry Monster Files*

40 *The Case of the Missing Bird Dog*

41 *The Case of the Shipwrecked Tree*

42 *The Case of the Burrowing Robot*

43 *The Case of the Twisted Kitty*

44 *The Dungeon of Doom*

45 *The Case of the Falling Sky*

46 *The Case of the Tricky Trap*

47 *The Case of the Tender Cheeping Chickies*

48 *The Case of the Monkey Burglar*

49 *The Case of the Booby-Trapped Pickup*

50 *The Case of the Most Ancient Bone*

51 *The Case of the Blazing Sky*

52 *The Quest for the Great White Quail*

53 *Drover's Secret Life*

54 *The Case of the Dinosaur Birds*

55 *The Case of the Secret Weapon*

56 *The Case of the Coyote Invasion*

57 *The Disappearance of Drover*

58 *The Case of the Mysterious Voice*

59 *The Case of the Perfect Dog*

60 *The Big Question*

61 *The Case of the Prowling Bear*

62 *The Ghost of Rabbits Past*

63 *The Return of the Charlie Monsters*

64 *The Case of the Three Rings*

65 *The Almost Last Roundup*

66 *The Christmas Turkey Disaster*

67 *Wagons West*

68 *The Secret Pledge*

69 *The Case of the Wandering Goats*

70 *The Case of the Troublesome Lady*

71 *The Case of the Monster Fire*

72 *The Case of the Three-Toed Tree Sloth*

73 *The Case of the Buried Deer*

74 *The Frozen Rodeo*

And, be sure to check out the
Audiobooks!

If you've never heard a *Hank the Cowdog* audiobook, you're missing out on a lot of fun! Each Hank book has also been recorded as an unabridged audiobook for the whole family to enjoy!

Praise for the Hank Audiobooks:

"It's about time the Lone Star State stopped hogging Hank the Cowdog, the hilarious adventure series about a crime solving ranch dog. Ostensibly for children, the audio renditions by author John R. Erickson are sure to build a cult following among adults as well." — *Parade Magazine*

"Full of regional humor . . . vocals are suitably poignant and ridiculous. A wonderful yarn." — *Booklist*

"For the detectin' and protectin' exploits of the canine Mike Hammer, hang Hank's name right up there with those of other anthropomorphic greats...But there's no sentimentality in Hank: he's just plain more rip-roaring fun than the others. Hank's misadventures as head of ranch security on a spread somewhere in the Texas Panhandle are marvelous situation comedy." — *School Library Journal*

"Knee-slapping funny and gets kids reading."

— *Fort Worth Star Telegram*

The Ranch Life Learning Series

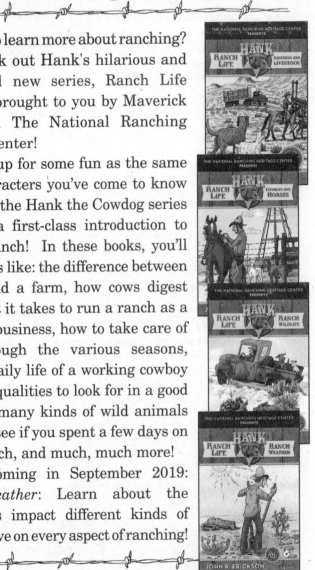

Want to learn more about ranching? Check out Hank's hilarious and educational new series, Ranch Life Learning, brought to you by Maverick Books and The National Ranching Heritage Center!

Saddle up for some fun as the same cast of characters you've come to know and love in the Hank the Cowdog series gives you a first-class introduction to life on a ranch! In these books, you'll learn things like: the difference between a ranch and a farm, how cows digest grass, what it takes to run a ranch as a successful business, how to take care of cattle through the various seasons, what the daily life of a working cowboy looks like, qualities to look for in a good horse, the many kinds of wild animals you might see if you spent a few days on Hank's ranch, and much, much more!

And, coming in September 2019: *Ranch Weather*: Learn about the tremendous impact different kinds of weather have on every aspect of ranching!

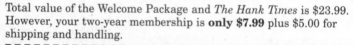

The following activities are samples from *The Hank Times*, the official newspaper of Hank's Security Force. Please do not write on these pages unless this is your book. And, even then, why not just find a scrap of paper?

"Rhyme Time"

W hat if Slim decides to give up his life as a ranch cowboy and go in search of other jobs? What kinds of jobs could he find?

Make a rhyme using "Slim" that would relate to his new job possibilities.

Example: Slim starts a tree trimming and removal business.

*Answer: Slim **LIMB**.*

1. Slim opens an aerobic dance studio.

2. Slim starts a line of cowboy hats known to keep the sun off your face.

3. Slim opens a barber shop.

4. Slim goes to locations building nests for bird homes.

G.L. Holmes

5. Slim becomes a church music leader.

6. Slim takes people on hikes along the Grand Canyon top.

7. Slim leads the US team's opponent.

8. Slim teaches people to be spontaneous and do things without really thinking.

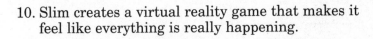

9. Slim can identity male criminals in lineups.

10. Slim creates a virtual reality game that makes it feel like everything is really happening.

11. Slim gets a job telling people when things are looking really bad.

12. Slim invents a switch that lowers the lights.

Answers:

1. Slim GYM
2. Slim BRIM
3. Slim TRIM
4. Slim LIMB
5. Slim HYMN
6. Slim RIM
7. Slim THEM
8. Slim WHIM
9. Slim HIM
10. Slim SIM
11. Slim GRIM
12. Slim DIM

"Word Maker"

T ry making up to twenty words from the letters in the names below. Use as many letters as possible, however, don't just add an "s" to a word you've already listed in order to have it count as another. Try to make up entirely new words for each line!

Then, count the total number of letters used in all of the words you made, and see how well you did using the Security Force Rankings below!

S L I M   C H A N C E

_____   _____

_____   _____

_____   _____

_____   _____

_____   _____

_____   _____

_____   _____

_____   _____

_____   _____

_____   _____

0 - 71 You spend too much time with J.T. Cluck and the chickens.

72 - 74 You are showing some real Security Force potential.

75 - 77 You have earned a spot on our Ranch Security team.

78 + Wow! You rank up there as a top-of-the-line cowdog.

"Photogenic" Memory Quiz

We all know that Hank has a "photogenic" memory—being aware of your surroundings is an important quality for a Head of Ranch Security. Now *you* can test your powers of observation.

How good is your memory? Look at the illustration on page 34 and try to remember as many things about it as possible. Then turn back to this page and see how many questions you can answer.

1. How many fence posts were there? 1, 2, or 3?

2. Were there any clouds in the sky?

3. How many steps were there? 1, 2, or 3?

4. Could you see a road anywhere?

5. Were both buzzards flying straight at you?

6. How many of Drover's eyes could you see? 1, 2, or all 3?

Have you visited Hank's official website yet?

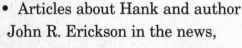

www.hankthecowdog.com

Don't miss out on exciting *Hank the Cowdog* games and activities, as well as up-to-date news about upcoming books in the series!

When you visit, you'll find:

• Hank's BLOG, which is the first place we announce upcoming books and new products!
• Hank's Official Shop, with tons of great *Hank the Cowdog* books, audiobooks, games, t-shirts, stuffed animals, mugs, bags, and more!
• Links to Hank's social media, whereby Hank sends out his "Cowdog Wisdom" to fans.
• A FREE, printable "Map of Hank's Ranch"!
• Hank's Music Page where you can listen to songs and even download FREE ringtones!
• A way to sign up for Hank's free email updates
• Sally May's "Ranch Roundup Recipes"!
• Printable & Colorable Greeting Cards for Holidays.
  • Articles about Hank and author John R. Erickson in the news,
  ...AND MUCH, MUCH MORE!

HANK
THE COWDOG

BOOKS
The Collection

FAN ZONE
Fun & Games

AUTHOR
Meet the Creator

STORE
Books & More

Find Toys, Games, Books & More at the Hank shop.

ANNOUNCING: A sneak peek at Hank #66

Hank Plays Cupid:

 GAMES
COME PLAY WITH HANK & PALS

 BOOKS
BROWSE THE ENTIRE HANK CATALOG

 FRIENDS
GET TO KNOW THE RANCH GANG

 Visit Hank's Facebook page

 Follow Hank on Twitter

 Watch Hank on YouTube

 Follow Hank on Pinterest

 Send Hank an Email

FROM THE BLOG

JAN 28 Hank is Cupid in Disguise...

JAN 18 The Valentine's Day Robbery! - a Snippet from the Story

DEC 04 Getting SIGNED Hank the Cowdog books for Christmas!

OCT 14 Education Association's lists of recommended books?

VISIT THE BLOG

 Hank's Survey
We'd love to know what you think! [GO]

TEACHER'S CORNER

Download fun activity guides, discussion questions and more.

SALLY MAY'S RECIPES

Discover delicious recipes from Sally May herself. [GO]

Hank's Music.
Free ringtones, music and more!

MORE

Official Shop
Find books, audio, toys and more!

 LET'S GO

Join Hank's Security Force
Get the activity letter and other cool stuff.

JOIN SECURITY FORCE

Get the Latest

Keep up with Hank's news and promotions by signing up for our e-news.

Looking for The Hank Times fan club newsletter?

[Enter your email address]
SIGN UP

Hank in the News

Find out what the media is saying about Hank. [GO]

FEATURED BOOK

The Christmas Turkey Disaster

Now Available!

Hank is in real trouble this time. L...

BUY   READ   LISTEN

Love Hank's Hilarious Songs?

Hank the Cowdog's "Greatest Hits" albums bring together the music from the unabridged audiobooks you know and love! These wonderful collections of hilarious (and sometimes touching) songs are unmatched. Where else can you learn about coyote philosophy, buzzard lore, why your dog is protecting an old corncob, how bugs compare to hot dog buns, and much more!

And, be sure to visit Hank's "Music Page" on the official website to listen to some of the songs and download FREE Hank the Cowdog ringtones!

MAVERICK BOOKS • 2 COMPACT DISCS
HANK THE COWDOG
Hank the Cowdog Greatest Hits, Volumes 1 & 2
Includes 45 Original Songs
SONGS WRITTEN BY
JOHN R. ERICKSON

2 COMPACT DISCS
Hank the Cowdog's Greatest Hits, Volumes 3 & 4
Includes 24 Original Songs
SONGS WRITTEN BY
JOHN R. ERICKSON

2 COMPACT DISCS
Hank the Cowdog's Greatest Hits, Volumes 5 & 6
SONGS WRITTEN BY
JOHN R. ERICKSON

"Audio-Only" Stories

Ever wondered what those "Audio-Only" Stories in Hank's Official Store are all about?

The Audio-Only Stories are Hank the Cowdog adventures that have never been released as books. They are about half the length of a typical Hank book, and there are currently seven of them. They have run as serial stories in newspapers for years and are now available as audiobooks!

We all know Hank loves to eat ... and now *you* can try some of his favorite recipes!

Have you visited Sally May's Kitchen yet?

http://www.hankthecowdog.com/recipes

Here, you'll find recipes for:

Sally May's Apple Pie

Hank's Picante Sauce

Round-Up Green Beans

Little Alfred's and Baby Molly's Favorite Cookies

Cowboy Hamburgers with Gravy

Chicken-Ham Casserole

...and MORE!

Teacher's Corner

Know a teacher who uses Hank in their classroom? You'll want to be sure they know about Hank's "Teacher's Corner"! Just click on the link on the homepage, and you'll find free teacher's aids, such as a printable map of Hank's ranch, a reading log, coloring pages, blog posts specifically for teachers and librarians, and much more!

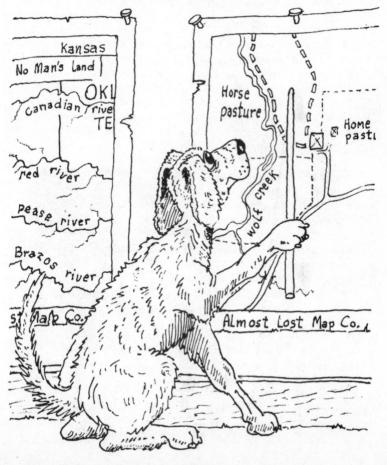

John R. Erickson,

a former cowboy, has written numerous books for both children and adults and is best known for his acclaimed *Hank the Cowdog* series. The *Hank* series began as a self-publishing venture in Erickson's garage in 1982 and has endured to become one of the nation's most popular series for children and families.

Through the eyes of Hank the Cowdog, a smelly, smart-aleck Head of Ranch Security, Erickson gives readers a glimpse into daily life on a cattle ranch in the West Texas Panhandle. His stories have won a number of awards, including the Audie, Oppenheimer, Wrangler, and Lamplighter Awards, and have been translated into Spanish, Danish, Farsi, and Chinese. *USA Today* calls the *Hank the Cowdog* books "the best family entertainment in years." Erickson lives and works on his ranch in Perryton, Texas, with his family.

Gerald L. Holmes

is a largely self-taught artist who grew up on a ranch in Oklahoma. For over thirty-five years, he has illustrated the *Hank the Cowdog* books and serial stories, as well as numerous other cartoons and textbooks, and his paintings have been featured in various galleries across the United States. He and his wife live in Perryton, Texas, where they raised their family, and where he continues to paint his wonderfully funny and accurate portrayals of modern American ranch life to this day.